D1368587

BOXED IN

BOXED IN
Mary Towne

THOMAS Y. CROWELL   New York

Copyright © 1982 by Mary Towne

All rights reserved. Printed in the United States of America. No part of this book may be
used or reproduced in any manner whatsoever without written permission except in the
case of brief quotations embodied in critical articles and reviews. For information address
Thomas Y. Crowell Junior Books, 10 East 53rd Street, New York, N.Y. 10022. Published
simultaneously in Canada by Fitzhenry & Whiteside Limited, Toronto.
Designed by Joyce Hopkins

Library of Congress Cataloging in Publication Data

Towne, Mary.
Boxed in.
SUMMARY: Kate goes through much deliberation and soul-
searching in trying to decide whether or not to give up her
beloved horse Tracker to her best friend Shelby.
    [1. Horses—Fiction.   2. Friendship—Fiction]   I. Title.
PZ7.S7473Bo   1982   [Fic]   81–43875
                              AACR2
ISBN 0-690-04239-6   ISBN 0-690-04240-X (lib. bdg.)

1 2 3 4 5 6 7 8 9 10

First Edition

BOXED IN

1

It's funny the way horses mostly won't eat wildflowers. All the way around the outside of the paddock fence there's a strip of cropped grass so smooth and even you'd think it was made by a lawnmower instead of by two horses stretching their necks under the top rail and chomping with their big teeth as far as they can reach. But between this strip and the dirt of the paddock, nestled along the bottom rail, there are fat clumps of buttercups that glisten in the sunshine. They look good enough to eat, even to me; but no, the horses never touch them. Same thing with the daisies just beginning to bloom in the field beyond the paddock, and, later on, the black-eyed Susans and the blue chicory. The horses just graze around them. Mom says it's very considerate of them, all those nice bouquets left there for the picking.

I came straight out to the paddock today after school. Usually, after the bus drops me off at the bottom of our driveway, I head for the house to dump my books and make myself a snack. Today I told myself I wasn't hungry—which isn't really true. Whatever happens, I can almost always eat. Like the horses, come to think of it. No, today I just didn't want to take the time. It feels as if I've been rushing all day just to get to this moment. And now that I'm finally here all I want to do is make time stand still.

Tracker ambles over to the fence and stands pricking his ears at me, hoping I'll grab him a mouthful of grass from beyond the bare strip he and John have made. Instead, to tease him, I pluck a handful of buttercups and hold them out to him. "Let's see if you like butter," I say, brushing them lightly under his hairy chin. Tracker tosses his head and backs away, looking at me so reproachfully that I can't help laughing. Tracker hates to be laughed at, it hurts his dignity. He turns around, showing me his shiny, dappled rump, and walks deliberately back toward his stall, passing John on the way—John, who's plodding over to me in his usual straight line, his big head hanging, telling me he doesn't expect much but would just as soon not be left out of anything that's going on. Even when he gets to the fence where I'm standing he doesn't raise his head. He just turns sideways and stares at the ground.

"Oh, John," I say, for probably the hundredth time, "why do you have to *look* like that?" As if he's just lost his best friend, my father always says. But John's best friend is only fifty yards away in his stall, making a big thing about chewing on some wisps of hay to show me he doesn't care about green grass anyway. I reach over the rail and run my fingers through a tangle in John's coarse brown mane, and find a couple of burrs. John stands patiently while I work them out. Maybe he doesn't even feel them.

Unlike Tracker, John has practically no nerves at all. If you laugh at him he just waits for you to stop laughing and do something else. The only things he's finicky about are his water bucket—he won't drink out of it if there's so much as a twig or a leaf in the water—and the place by the power line where he was once scared by a rabbit bounding across the trail ahead of him. You'd think he'd remember things like bulldozers and motorcycles and yapping dogs, but no—it's a little cottontail rabbit that's got stuck in his big, dim, cloudy brain. Like an elephant and a mouse, maybe. Anyhow, you still have to make a detour around that spot. Only yesterday—

5

But I don't want to think about yesterday, or why I was riding John again instead of Tracker. Most of all I don't want to think about last night. I'd rather think safe, familiar thoughts, such as why horses don't like wildflowers, or whether there's another fencepost around to replace the one I'm leaning on, which I notice has a long splintery crack in it.

Because sooner or later John will notice the crack too, and begin leaning against the post for a few hours at a time, until finally it gives way and he can go down to the pond and stuff himself on the lush green grass that grows there. Not that getting John back is ever any problem. In spite of all the time and effort he spends trying to find a way out of the paddock he never seems to make the vital connection between getting out and staying out. You can walk right up to him and loop a rope around his neck, and he'll plod meekly at your heels all the way back up the hill to his stall.

But if Tracker gets out too, that's a real hassle. He never seems to have a definite destination, like John, and the longer he stays out the jumpier he gets, as if he doesn't really know what to do with his freedom. He'll trot halfway down the driveway and then wheel around and come galloping back as if something's chasing him. Or he'll browse for a while in the upper field we use for hay, raising his head nervously from time to time as if he thinks he's on the plains of Africa, with maybe a lion lurking among the maple trees. Sometimes he'll give a snort and go cantering around in a circle and then make a sudden run at the stone wall that borders our property there. This makes me clench my fists and pray, thinking of all the scattered, broken boulders on the far side of the wall. But of course he always draws up short at the last moment, blowing and tossing his head.

Anyhow, the only way to catch Tracker is to pretend you don't care if he comes or not. An apple or a carrot usually helps, once you've managed to get close enough to show it to him, but still you have to keep playing it cool. You have to shrug your shoulders and turn away, sauntering along casually as if you weren't listening for the sound of him swishing through the long grass behind you. Even when you can feel his warm breath whoofing against the back of your neck you have to act as though you don't know he's anywhere near . . . until you finally get to the paddock gate. Then you can grab him and send him through with a slap on his rump, telling him exactly what you think of him.

Only then, of course, you have to give him the apple or carrot, which he accepts as if it's only his due. Meanwhile old John, who was the cause of the whole hassle in the first place, looks at you sadly, wondering why you didn't bring him a treat too.

Horses are such characters. I know that a lot of

people—Pam for one (and Shelby too? . . . no, don't think about Shelby, not just yet)—see them mainly in terms of riding: their gaits, the kind of schooling they've had, their bloodlines, their color and conformation, and all that. To them a horse's personality is made up of practical things like how willing he is, whether he spooks easily, if he has good stable manners. But to me they're animals first and horses second, if you know what I mean. The people we got Tracker from kept telling us what a good horse he was—meaning his half-Arabian blood, his quick responses, the clean way he takes a fence—and that was fine with me; I'd outgrown my old pony and was ready for a good horse, and besides, at the price we were paying, I knew Tracker had better be good.

It was really Tracker the animal I fell in love with, though—with the look of intelligence in his bright, dark eyes and the strong curve of his neck under the palm of my hand; with the way he gently stamped the ground from time to time as if to say he was tired of standing around waiting for all these humans to finish staring at him, but was too polite to do anything about it just yet. Mom said he reminded her of a wooden horse she'd had as a kid, painted dapple-gray with a dark mane and tail like Tracker's. "He's so . . . sort of *cute*," she said—which certainly wasn't the right word, but I knew what she meant. People tend to smile when they look at Tracker. That's the best way I can explain it.

People including horse-show judges, maybe. Even when they're supposed to be watching for things like a collected canter, or a smooth change of lead. . . .

It looks like I've come to the end of my safe thoughts in spite of myself. Judges, shows—I told myself I wasn't going to think about any of that, not now, not here. But of course I have to, for Tracker's sake. It's Tracker-the-good-horse I have to consider now. I have to do what's best for him. I know. I know. *But what about me?*

I lean against the fence, feeling the June sunshine warm and slippery on the top of my head. I can hear the phone ringing faintly in the house behind me, and Mom's impatient exclamation as she leaves her weeding in the side flowerbed to go answer it. In the big pear tree by the garage, a mockingbird stops trying to sound like a robin and starts imitating a cardinal instead. Tracker is still just a dim shape inside the dark rectangle of his stall, but John has moved to the section of fence that overlooks the long green slope of the field and is staring at the grass fixedly, willing me to let him out to graze. I have to grin at the way he's standing—motionless, not even swishing his tail at the flies, his whole body locked into the one desire. Statue of a big brown horse thinking: grass.

I look at my watch. Quarter to four. I could let

9

the horses out into the field for an hour or so before their supper, and cut down on Tracker's feed accordingly. It's only Tuesday. Tomorrow will be soon enough to start his special rations for the weekend.

Maybe I'll go in and change my clothes before I let the horses out. There's some brush in the far corner of the field that needs cutting down. It's probably where John got his burrs. I could get the big shears and do some work on it before I start my homework. Besides, I love being in the field when the horses are there, listening to the dry tearing sound of their teeth as they pull at the grass and the shuffle of their hooves as they change position, shifting slowly from place to place. I like the good, rich smell of their coats warming in the sun. Without even looking at them, I can share their contentment and peace. And it will be the same again today. . . . Won't it?

My schoolbooks are still lying in a heap at my feet where I dumped them. As I stoop to pick them up I hear footsteps behind me. I know who it is without turning. She must have cut across the grass instead of coming up the track, or I'd have heard her before.

"Hi," Shelby says. "Have you decided yet?" Her voice is bright, false, as if she were asking me a question about clothes, or what movie to see. I straighten, clutching the books to me, not turning to look at her. In a different tone, subdued, she says, "Or shouldn't I ask?"

"You shouldn't ask."

"Oh. Well, sorry. The way you were standing there . . . I thought maybe you were making up your mind."

Still I don't look at her. I can't. It wasn't so bad seeing her on the bus today, or at school, but here— Is Shelby going to keep on acting like nothing has changed between us? Well, to be fair, maybe from her point of view nothing has. We've both known it was coming, after all, even if we never really talked about it. The fact that her father called up last night with a definite offer just made it official, that's all.

"He could still stay here, you know," Shelby says. "I mean, you'd still be able to ride him and every-thing."

Gee thanks, I want to say. And like when? Where? My heavy science book has slithered out of my arms, and I bend down again to pick it up. "I need time to think about it," I mutter at last. "I told your father that."

"Sure. I know. But Kate—"

"Shelby, stop it!" I whirl around to glare at her. "I don't want to talk about it right now, can't you understand? So just stop leaning on me. *Just leave it alone for now, can't you?*"

11

2

When we were younger people used to think Shelby and I were twins, or sisters at least; we were always having to explain that we were no relation. "Mirror images, maybe," Shelby's mother said once, pointing out that I part my hair on the right, and Shelby on the left; also that I'm right-handed, and Shelby left-handed. But in the last couple of years my mirror has changed, or at least the lighting has. My hair, which used to be almost ash-blonde, has darkened to a kind of streaky beige color, which makes my eyes look darker too. They were never as blue as Shelby's anyway, and now you notice the gray more than the blue. I'm taller than Shelby now, and my face seems to have stretched out too, so it's longer and thinner. It's not too bad a face, I don't think, but you can't exactly call it pretty.

When Shelby looks in her mirror she still sees the delicate pointed chin and rounded cheekbones we both used to have, and of course the blue eyes. The light in her mirror shimmers on silky real-blonde hair and gleams on a set of perfect white teeth. (For a while it was her braces that gleamed. I still have a gap between my front teeth, but naturally it was Shelby, whose teeth were always small and straight and even, who had to have orthodontia.) Even her skin seems to kind of hold the light. She never does get as dark a tan as I do, only a sort of gold color, as if the sun knows exactly when to stop. We both wash our faces three times a day with Noxzema, but if Shelby ever gets a pimple it's in a place where you hardly notice it, like under her chin or up next to her hairline.

And when Shelby dresses up to ride in a show, wearing her dark blue velvet habit (or in hot weather a linen-weave coat in a lighter shade of blue), with her shining hair clubbed back just so, she looks just like one of the rich country-club kids from down around the shore, places like Westport and Darien and Greenwich. Or maybe even more so, if you know what I mean—as if she went to the very best private school of them all, and never had to wash the dishes at home, and spent all her vacations in places like Bermuda and Nassau, and could have been a junior tennis champion if she hadn't decided to concentrate on riding instead.

Which is kind of funny when you think about it, because between the two of us I guess you'd have to say that I'm the one who's always been the rich kid. Not that we are—rich, I mean. But compared to Shelby's family . . . well, our house isn't anything fancy, it's just a farmhouse, but it is quite big. Even if I wasn't an only child I wouldn't have had to share a room the way Shelby's always done, until this year when her oldest sister Karen got married and left home. (Her other sisters, Donna and Molly, are still griping about Shelby getting to have the room to herself now, even though she's the youngest. Shelby just shrugs and says possession is nine points of the law, which makes my father, who's a lawyer, grin.)

Anyway, the Petersons' house is just an ordinary-size Cape set close to the road, with a small side yard, and the woods pressing up against it from behind. When Shelby first came up here to play—we were in kindergarten then, or maybe first grade—she acted as if our house was practically a palace, and our ten acres some kind of foreign kingdom. In fact, she was a little shy at first. She wasn't used to so much space, inside or out. When I'd go running off through one of the fields Shelby would hang back, picking her way along gingerly, worrying about snakes and grasshoppers and getting burrs in her socks, and I don't know what all. She wouldn't go into the barn for ages because of the cobwebs and the shadowy rafters and the swallows swooping in and out like bats.

She wasn't used to animals, either. We had three dogs then, and although she tried not to show she was scared of them, you could tell she was by the way she'd stand very still with her fists clenched by her sides while they sniffed around her, wagging their tails. Even our two black barn cats made her nervous. They weren't cute and cuddly, the way she thought cats were supposed to be. Instead they prowled around the place like miniature panthers, and were apt to scratch if you tried to pick them up. We also had a pet goose named Barnaby, who didn't like strangers—or anybody much, to tell the truth—and who would sometimes charge at Shelby with his wings flapping and his beak outstretched. Those were the only times Shelby ever cried, but I didn't blame her for being scared of Barnaby. We all were, a little, and weren't too sorry when something—a fox, probably—got him one spring night.

But in the course of time, Shelby made friends with the dogs and learned to leave the cats alone, and got to feel almost as much at home in the house and barn and fields as I was. Then, the summer I was eight, I got my Welsh pony, Max. It's strange to remember how I practically had to beg Shelby to get up on Max for the first time. And not just the first time: it was weeks before Shelby would relax and stop clutching his mane, even though Max was only walking slowly round and round the paddock while I led him. If I managed to coax her—and Max—into trying a trot, Shelby would bite her lip and look brave. After jouncing around for a minute or so she'd say that she thought she really liked just walking better.

I'd had a few riding lessons at a small academy on the edge of town, but now that I had my own pony my parents got one of the girls who taught there to come give me some lessons at home. At first we just stayed in the paddock, but pretty soon we moved out into the front field, which is the only one that's level enough to be any good for riding. My father mowed a big ring in the grass, and later, when I got Tracker, we put up some jumps—not the fancy white gates that are there now, just homemade ones put together out of old tires and barrels and fence rails.

(We call it the front field, but actually it's across the road. And it doesn't belong to us, we only lease it from Mr. Clayborne, who owns—or used to own—most of the land on that side. Dad tried to buy it for years to protect our view over the valley, but Mr. Clayborne would never sell. And of course now that it *is* finally for sale, it's at a price we can't possibly afford.)

Anyway, sometimes Shelby would sit on the fence and watch while I was learning to trot and canter and keep my heels down and my elbows in, but usually she'd get bored and wander off on her own. That next winter, which was a long, cold one, she'd sometimes come out to the barn with me while I gave Max his evening feed; but in the mornings, when I'd get on the school bus with my lips still blue and my fingers all numb and chapped and red from trying to break the ice in Max's water bucket, she'd just shake her head and say she didn't know why anyone would want a horse, they were so much trouble.

I don't know what changed her mind. It might have been the Madison Square Garden horse show we saw on TV, or the revival of *National Velvet* my mother took us to one Saturday over in Danbury, or all the horse books I was always pressing Shelby to read. Partly, I guess, it was my new friend Ellen. Because by spring I wasn't spending as much time with Shelby as I had before. Now that I'd had a few more lessons my parents said I could ride Max away from home, as long as I didn't go too far and had someone to ride with.

And so I met Ellen, who lived a mile or so up the road. She was two years older than me and had a real horse, not just a pony, but her parents had the same rule about not riding alone. (In fact, Mom still isn't very happy when I go off on my own for more than an hour or two. Not that I do much any more.) There weren't any regular bridle trails of course, but there were still plenty of dirt roads then, and lots of open fields. So Ellen and I went riding together almost every day after school, and Shelby was jealous. I tried to explain that Ellen was okay, but that she was older and just a riding friend anyway, not a best friend. But I could tell Shelby's feelings were hurt by the way she put her chin in the air and shrugged and said, "Oh, I don't mind," in the sugar-sweet voice she always uses when she's fibbing.

Anyhow, you could have knocked me over with a feather, or at least a curry comb, when I found out what Shelby had asked for as her main birthday present that year: riding lessons. And not only lessons, but also a hard hat like mine, and boots (mine were second-hand, but Shelby got new ones), and even a crop. Both her parents worked, but her sister Karen had just gotten her driver's license, so every Wednesday afternoon Karen drove Shelby over to the little riding academy for an hour's lesson.

Naturally I was delighted, even though Shelby didn't talk about it much. Then, after about six weeks had gone by, she asked me one day if she could ride Max. "Just in the paddock, I mean." I said sure, and hung on the fence to watch while Shelby put Max

18

through his paces, such as they were. Shelby's always been a quick learner, but I was really impressed by the way she handled Max in that confined space. The paddock's long and narrow, which makes the turns very tight, especially at a canter. It's the safest kind of space for a beginner because the horse can't bolt, he's always brought up short by the fence.

But Shelby didn't seem like a beginner, even then. It wasn't so much that she did things right—carefully, almost too carefully, remembering everything she'd been taught—as that she just somehow *looked* right on a horse. Her movements are naturally neat and firm, and with her straight back and slender shoulders and that special lift of her chin, she has what I guess you'd call style. She almost made Max look stylish—old roly-poly Max, with his barrel sides and stubby legs. I've noticed since then that even when Shelby is a bit tense (and I think she's secretly still a little scared of horses) she somehow makes you want to go on watching her. Sort of like Tracker, in that way. And maybe that little bit of fear makes her try even harder—makes her extra alert and aware of what she's doing every second.

But at the time, of course, all I was really thinking about was how much fun Shelby and I were going to have riding together—or if not together, at least taking turns on Max. I said she could come up and ride him any time, and why couldn't she have Pam

19

come and give her lessons here, the way I'd done? It wouldn't cost any more, and I was sure it would be okay with my parents. Besides, Max needed all the exercise he could get to keep him from getting any fatter.

Shelby thought about it for a minute, and then shook her head. "Pam's going to let me ride Dandy next week," she said. "He has a really super trot, and when you canter he knows how to change leads and everything. I mean, Max is nice, but . . ."

We both looked at Max, who was blissfully munching on a big bunch of parsley I'd brought him from the vegetable garden. Max was crazy about parsley for some reason. He looked pretty silly, with the bright green fronds hanging out of his mouth. Besides which, I knew him for the lazy, stubborn pony he was. He could change leads all right, but only if he happened to be in the mood. Ellen had let me ride her Morgan a couple of times, and I knew Shelby was right: she'd learn a lot more, about proper riding at least, on a well-schooled horse than she would just bouncing around on Max. But I couldn't help feeling a little hurt.

"Well, sure," I said. "But gosh, just riding around and around in that dinky little ring . . . there isn't any place to *go*. I mean, they don't even have any trails."

"But that's how you learn," Shelby said, looking

at me earnestly. "In the ring, where the teacher can watch you."

I thought of my long, aimless rambles through the summer fields, of the shady dirt road where Ellen and I had once seen a doe and her fawn grazing at the edge of some woods, of the creek where we'd tie the horses to a tree and take off our boots and sit dangling our feet in the cool, brown water—and knew I wouldn't trade my kind of riding for going around in circles inside somebody's white-painted fence, even on a horse with a super trot.

That was almost four years ago, before the town began to change, before Shelby got John and I got Tracker, before Shelby's father got into the act. But I guess you could say the pattern was set right then and there.

3

I didn't mean to yell at Shelby, but I guess I did.

She stands staring at me, trim and neat in her week-day riding clothes—no crummy old jeans for Shelby any more, she wears a tailored shirt with tan knit breeches and low boots—looking stunned. Hurt, even.

Is she putting it on? No. She really doesn't understand how I feel. She starts to say something, then thinks better of it. Instead, she gives a little shrug. "Well, okay, sure. If that's the way you want it. I guess I couldn't help hoping . . . but anyway."

"Did you expect me to be *pleased*?" I ask incredulously. I probably sound as if I'm trying to give her a hard time, but I'm not; I really want to know.

"Well, no, not exactly. But I thought you'd—you know—feel better having things settled. I guess I thought we had a kind of agreement—"

"We didn't," I interrupt. "And things *aren't* settled."

"Okay, okay, I get the message," Shelby says lightly; but her blue eyes still look hurt. "I didn't mean to make you mad, Kate, honestly." When I don't answer, she touches my arm and gives me her best smile. "We won't talk about it at all if you don't want to. Just . . . business as usual. Right?"

"Right," I agree, trying to match her tone and her smile.

But there's an awkward little silence. Together we turn back to the fence. John hasn't even cocked an ear in Shelby's direction—he's still staring out at the field, waiting for me to come around and open the gate on that side. But Tracker, attracted by the sound of our voices, has left his stall and is walking springily toward us. I'm not imagining it, there really is something extra in his step when Shelby's around, as if he's always showing off for her a little. She reaches out a hand and strokes his nose absently, and he rolls his eyes at me. Playing us off against each other as usual, I think. The thought no longer makes me want to smile.

I look again at Shelby's clothes and say, "I didn't think you were going to ride today. I was just about to let the horses out in the field."

"I wasn't, but Mr. Burroughs gave us an extension on our English paper, it's not due till Thursday now." She sighs. "Only six more days of school. Boy, will I be glad when it's over."

We both know this isn't really true, it's just one of those things you're supposed to say. Shelby's a straight-A student and one of the most popular kids in our class. Which is funny in a way, because she certainly doesn't go out of her way to be friendly. It's partly her looks, I guess, and the cool way she does everything, sort of casual but efficient. She makes people want her to notice them. Next year at this time she'll probably be walking away with half the awards at eighth-grade graduation.

"Anyway," she says, "I'd like to get in an hour on the jumps now. It's supposed to rain tomorrow, and if it does it'll mean only one more workout, on Thursday. Pam's bringing the van over right after school on Friday so we can get an early start," she explains. "There'll probably be a lot of weekend traffic, and besides, if we get there soon enough, we can have dinner with the people we're staying with. Never miss a free meal if you can help it, Pam says. If that's okay with you, taking him that early?" she adds. Usually this wouldn't be a real question, it'd be just politeness.

24

Today she gives me an anxious look.

I nod automatically. Actually, I've already tuned out most of what she's been saying. I don't want to hear about the show, which is in New York State and is the biggest one—or at least the most important—Shelby's ridden in so far. I don't want to hear about Pam or about which other horses she's taking, and what classes they're entered in, and what their chances are. Instead I find myself thinking about rain tomorrow, which doesn't seem possible on this cloudless June afternoon. But I should have noticed before: a day this clear and windless, with a sky so blue it hurts your eyes, often turns out to be what the local people (the few real locals that are left) call a weatherbreeder. By morning it will be as if someone has drawn a big gray shade across the sky; as if one glimpse of a perfect day is all you're allowed at a time.

Shelby goes off to the barn, striding briskly along the fence past the buttercups, saying, "Come on, boy," over her shoulder. But Tracker doesn't really need any urging. He pretends to crop at a weed as a token show of resistance, but then raises his head and looks after her. In another moment he is moving obediently toward his stall. With me, saddling Tracker has always been something of a game. He'll come eventually, but he has to have his joke first. Lately it hasn't even been that much of a joke. It hurts to admit it, but I know it's only Tracker's good manners, the years of

25

obedience to human will, that make him stand still for me. I always feel he's looking over my shoulder for Shelby.

Well, what do I expect? With me on his back Tracker knows he's in for cars and trucks and bulldozers, for loud noises and bad smells and metal under his feet, with maybe one good gallop before the return trip if we're lucky. With Shelby, he gets to do what he was bred for.

I turn away from the fence with my armload of books. "Sorry, John," I say—meaning the grazing—but John has already given up, he's lumbering around to face the other way, hanging his head again. He knows he's not allowed out in the field while Tracker's being ridden. In the paddock, he'll only nicker and whinny and move restlessly along the fence, wanting his friend back. But in the field he acts like a crazy colt, galloping around in all directions—moving faster, in fact, than you can ever get him to go when you're riding him—so that we're always afraid he'll put a foot in a rabbit hole and hurt himself. Once he jumped the stone wall right into my mother's rose garden. Mom was mad about her roses, but I was mainly amazed that John would actually jump over anything more than two feet high, which is his usual limit.

I cross the back lawn, where Mom's straw hat and trowel and weeding fork are lying on the grass. I find her in the kitchen making herself a glass of iced tea.

"Want some?" she asks as I dump my books on the table. I shake my head. She looks at me and sighs. "Well, I might as well tell you the bad news right now. That call was from Alice Meeker"—Mrs. Meeker is a neighbor of ours—"saying that the front field has been sold. To a developer. Well, we've known it was coming. But still. . . ."

But still. At first, when old Mr. Clayborne sold his house and moved to Florida—having sold all but a few plots out of the hundred acres his family had owned for generations—we hoped the new people might decide to buy the field too. It's the closest one to the house, and we thought they might want it for privacy. But either they didn't care about privacy or, more likely, just couldn't afford the price, and the field stayed on the market. Then we hoped that maybe it would be bought by someone, a rich someone, who'd just put up a single house and leave the rest of the land open. But as Dad said, that was hoping for the moon. Even with the two-acre zoning the town voted in a few years ago, a developer could put up three houses there, maybe four if he got permission to use fill in the lower part that gets swampy every spring.

Mom probably hates the thought of those houses even more than I do; but I can tell from the look of worry and concern on her face that it's mainly me she's thinking of.

I manage a shrug. "Oh, well. As far as riding goes . . . it's mostly Shelby who uses the field now, anyway. All it means is that if I do decide to sell Tracker"— I swallow hard—"she'll have to board him somewhere else. It's what she really wants to do anyway. At Pam's, probably, or maybe over at the academy, if they have room. Someplace where he'll have a nice big box stall and maybe be allowed out to graze once a week for half an hour. You know, all his feed measured out scientifically, right down to the last teaspoon, and a bath every other day."

I can't keep the bitterness out of my voice, and Mom looks so distressed that I'm immediately sorry. She's such a comfortable, relaxed kind of mother— not like Shelby's mother, Mrs. Peterson, who's always dieting and changing her hair color and taking courses in aerobic dancing and Chinese cooking and I don't know what all, as if she's afraid to let herself alone— that it gives you a funny feeling to see her taking something so hard.

I say, "It's okay, Mom, really. It would probably be easier for me anyway, not having him stay here."

Is this true? I really don't know. Mom just looks at me for a minute and then says softly, "If you decide to keep him, Kate, maybe we can do something about the back field. The hay won't be worth that much anyway by the time we finish paying someone for baling it. If we can even find anyone to do the baling, now that Ed Dayton's moving upstate." She pauses, and I know she's wondering what will happen to the Dayton farm, which is the last one of any size in our area. A corporate headquarters, or maybe condominiums?

"Anyhow," she continues, "we'd never be able to make it into a proper dressage ring—not that you care about that anyway—but if we got a bulldozer in I'm sure we could level it off enough so that you could ride there."

"No more bulldozers!" I can hear my voice beginning to crack. "And riding around and around in a little circle? No thanks."

I turn away blindly. "Kate!" Mom says in a sharp voice that she hardly ever uses. "You've got to realize that for the last year or so it's Shelby who's been giving Tracker his exercise. If you keep him, and Shelby buys another horse, it's going to be your responsibility to keep him in shape. And you can't do that by just hacking him around town. You'll need a place to ride, in little circles if necessary."

"I *have* places to ride!" I shout. "There are still the fields beyond the elementary school, and the power line, and Munson's woods, and Bayberry Lane—they haven't paved that yet. In fact, the people there don't want it paved, some of them anyway, they're getting up a petition—"

Suddenly my throat is choked with tears. Mom puts

29

a hand on my shoulder, but I shake it off. I have to be alone. I start through the dining room to the hall, heading for the front porch where there's an old glider swing I like to sit on when I'm upset or mad or need to think about something. But from there I'll have to see Shelby putting Tracker through his paces in the field across the road, taking him elegantly over the high white jumps, and today I don't think I can stand that. I hesitate in the hall, and Tess, our old collie, who's lying on the rug there, raises her narrow graying muzzle at me and swishes her tail, waiting to be patted.

Instead I turn away and go slowly up the narrow farmhouse stairs to my room, which is at the back of the house. It's flooded with afternoon sunlight, and suddenly I can't bear to be shut up inside after all. I shove open the window that looks out on the paddock, where John is moseying along the fence and whinnying for Tracker, and then the other window overlooking the rose bed and the long slope of lawn leading down to the pond. But almost immediately a chain saw starts up its giant-mosquito whine in the woods on the other side—another tree going down to make room for another fake Colonial, or maybe a split-level with a cathedral ceiling. I slam both windows shut again. My eye is caught by a dusty blue-silk ribbon taped to the mirror, a souvenir of a Pony Club rally two years ago, the first and last I ever rode in. I rip it off and fling it into the wastebasket, and then flop down on my bed and stare up at the light rippling like water across the ceiling.

Maybe that was my weather-breeder, I think suddenly: those first few golden years of having Tracker. And now everything is just going to be gray for a long time, as far ahead as I can see.

4

"Listen, Kate, I think you should hang in there. I mean, if it means that much to you . . . and this other kid, this so-called friend of yours, she'll just go out and buy some other horse anyway, right? Like she doesn't care about the horse himself, just as long as he does his thing and she can bring home another ribbon—right?"

It's the next day. Instead of going straight home from school, I got the bus driver to let me off within walking distance of my friend Larry's—the place some people call the Zoo because it's a kind of commune,

32

or mini-commune, or at least not lived in by a regular family; though sometimes I think the people there are more of a family than some real families I know.

It's a big old Victorian house, not far from the center of town, with lots of the fancy wooden trim that's called gingerbread. It's crumbling like gingerbread too since the owner, Mrs. Kirby, won't spend any money for repairs, and Larry says they've never yet had anyone to stay who was a good enough carpenter to replace all the missing wooden scallops and twirly bedpost knobs. In fact the whole place looks pretty rundown, at least from the front, because of the way the porch sags and the grass has been allowed to grow up tall. The long grass is on purpose, though—Larry says lawns are poor ecology.

No one ever sees around back, where there's a fantastic vegetable garden, something growing on practically every square inch of space, and all of it as carefully tended as most people's living rooms. If people did see the garden maybe they'd feel differently about Larry and his friends. But it's completely surrounded by a high board fence that even the neighborhood kids haven't figured a way over. Larry says it's for privacy and to protect the garden, but some people say it's because he grows marijuana there. I don't know, maybe he does; I don't know what it looks like, and I've never asked.

Anyhow, most of the bad feeling against the place

has died down in the last year or so, partly because people decided it was really Mrs. Kirby who was to blame—and Mrs. Kirby doesn't care about blame, all she cares about is rent money—and partly because Larry and his friends have never caused the kind of trouble everyone seemed to expect, whatever that was. Wild parties, I guess, or nude sunbathing on the front porch, or maybe begging with tin cups on Main Street. As a matter of fact, most of the regular members have ordinary jobs, except for Rita, who's a weaver, and Larry himself. He likes to switch from one thing to another, and when he's earned enough money to get by on for a while he just quits and relaxes until the money runs out. Then he finds another job. I don't know, in some ways it seems like a sensible way to live.

Of course there are still some people, like Mr. and Mrs. Peterson, who think it's terrible for people to live together if they aren't related or married to each other. Luckily my parents don't feel that way; and ever since the day last summer when I was trying to get Tracker to cross the railroad tracks and Larry stopped his old panel truck to see if he could help (he couldn't) I've considered him one of my best friends. I like the others too, but Larry is special.

Today he's pleased because it's raining, which is good for the new seedlings in the garden, and also gives him a day off from his current job as a housepainter. He throws me a dishtowel to mop myself off with, and then leads me into the big, bare front room because he can see right away that I want to talk. (I try not to notice that the dish towel is pretty grubby, and only hope Larry won't hang it back up on the kitchen rack. The indoor housekeeping isn't exactly up to the standard of the outdoor housekeeping, but with so little furniture you don't notice the dust too much.)

I sit down on one of the big floor cushions and watch while Larry builds a fire in the marble-faced fireplace. It really is chilly in here, and I can't help thinking that if there were curtains at the tall windows instead of just shades the room would at least look warmer. But I guess curtains would just be something else to get dusty. Larry himself is barefoot, as usual, and wearing just a T-shirt with his jeans. I know the fire is for my benefit; he never seems to feel the cold even though he's skinny.

Larry is in his early thirties, I think, with reddish hair and a darker red beard and bright gray eyes behind gold-rimmed glasses that right now are spattered with paint. After my parents first met him, I said it was hard to believe he grew up in a rich town like New Canaan and went to prep school and an Ivy League college and everything; but my father smiled a little sadly and said it wasn't hard at all.

After he gets the fire going Larry sits down next

35

to the fireplace with his back against the wall and his legs outstretched, ready to listen, and I start telling him about my problem with Tracker and Shelby. Last night, before I finally got to sleep, I decided Larry would be a good person to talk to because he thinks about things differently from most people. I don't mean just his opinions, I mean the way he thinks— questioning ideas that most people take for granted, and never saying things like, "Oh, well, you can't beat the system," or "That's life."

But I'm bothered by the way he seems to be putting Shelby down, calling her my so-called friend.

"Well, it's not quite like that," I tell him. "I mean, I don't know how Shelby would feel about another horse, but she really does love Tracker. And when she's riding him, it's—I don't know, it's like they fit together. Not just the way they look, I mean, but the way they kind of understand each other."

This last part is hard for me to say, but Larry only raises his eyebrows and goes back to what I said first. "She doesn't love him like you do, though," he says, not asking, just stating a fact.

I shake my head. For a moment I can't speak. But what's the point of coming all the way over here in the first place if all I'm going to do is cry? I take a deep breath and try to explain, going back to the beginning.

"The thing is, Tracker's a good horse. He's even

better than we thought he was when we got him. That's mainly because of all the time Shelby's spent working with him." There's no point in not being honest, either. "But to begin with—well, I just wanted a better horse than my pony, one that could jump and had good gaits and wasn't thinking about grass all the time. And Pam, my teacher—she's the one that's coaching Shelby now—said I was too good a rider not to have a good horse. Nothing fancy, but a horse that would at least challenge me. In fact, it was Pam who helped us find Tracker. I'm not bragging"—I look at Larry anxiously—"but in some ways I think I'm a better rider than Shelby. I'm more of an all-around rider, if you know what I mean."

He nods. "But not a show rider."

"No. I don't like it. When we got Tracker one of our ideas was that he'd be good for Pony Club. You don't ride just any old pony for Pony Club," I explain. "In fact there're a lot more horses than ponies, and some of them are really super. It sounds crazy, I know, but . . . Well, anyway, I thought Pony Club sounded like fun. You know, a chance to get to know some of the other kids around who had horses, and just fool around with them, and maybe learn something too. I thought it would be a casual kind of deal, you know?"

I shake my head. "But it wasn't like that at all. You had to do everything just so, there was all this boring dressage work, and you even had to go to night meetings at someone's house. And then there are these rallies they have, everyone has a rally level, and you ride against other Pony Club teams, and—well, it's sort of complicated to explain, but after a while it seemed as if all anyone ever thought about was their rally level. Parents too. They'd pay for extra lessons, they'd even buy a better horse, just so their kid could get a better rally level."

I stare into the bright flames, seeing not only those Pony Club sessions but some of the regular shows I went to when Shelby first started riding in them—the tense, pale faces of the riders waiting for their events to be called, the tears afterwards. I saw one girl throw up before a class, she was so scared. Another had a pony that kept refusing the same jump and got disqualified, and she began beating him with her crop until someone stopped her. And always the parents, almost as tense and nervous as the kids. One woman waited for her daughter to come out of the ring—she hadn't won a ribbon, or something—and then grabbed the horse's bridle and started yelling at her, pointing out everything the poor kid had done wrong, not even caring that everyone around could hear. The girl was fat, I remember, with her hair in braids, and she just sat there, trapped up high on her horse for everyone to stare at, with tears rolling down her face.

Shelby says I only see what I want to see, and that I pay more attention to the losers than I do to the winners. Maybe so. But since Shelby herself is usually a winner maybe *she* only sees what she wants to see.

"Anyway," I tell Larry, "I'd paid my dues and gone to all those meetings so I figured I might as well ride in the first rally, and I did, and our team won, and then I quit. Shelby thought I was crazy. She was dying to be in Pony Club herself, but she couldn't because all she had was John."

"John?"

"Shelby's horse, that she got just before I got Tracker."

Larry peers at me through his paint-spattered glasses. "You mean she already has a horse of her own? Well, for Pete's sake, why can't she ride him instead of ripping off yours?"

I have to laugh at the thought of John in a show ring, doubtfully eyeing a two-foot jump. Then I feel sad all over again, remembering how excited Shelby was when she first got John. She'd been bugging her parents for months to buy her a horse. Dad had said she could board it with us—he could easily box in another stall, and wouldn't charge her for hay, only for grain. It would be good for Max (or my new horse, when I got him) to have company, especially through the long winters when a horse by itself always seems so forlorn, standing around with nothing to look at but snow. As for the care involved, maybe Shelby could come up and do the evening grooming and feeding, while I took care of the mornings.

And that's the way it worked out. Shelby's parents finally gave in, and on her tenth birthday—a year after she'd started riding lessons—they answered an ad in the local paper. "Brown gelding, 15.4 hands, good trail horse, rides English or Western." That was John. As I explain to Larry, if you know anything about horse ads, that means just plain horse, in other words a hack, and you can only hope he's sound. Which John was (is), and not too bad-looking either, at least when he holds his head up. He seemed so big next to Max that I was a little in awe of him at first. In fact, when we heard about Tracker a few weeks later, and before we went to look at him, my first reaction was disappointment that he wasn't going to be as tall as John. (Actually, Tracker's only half a hand shorter, but so well-proportioned that he looks smaller.)

We had a great time that summer. Shelby would dutifully put John through his paces in the front field—there weren't any jumps there yet, only the wide ring—but after that we'd just take off over the countryside. I showed her all the places I'd ridden with Ellen (who had moved away), and we found some new ones as well. Tracker tended to be a bit spooky going along the roads, but John's plodding company seemed to soothe him; and besides, you didn't have

40

to use the roads all that much in those days. There were plenty of cross-country shortcuts you could take to wherever you wanted to go.

So we'd amble along, talking about whatever came into our heads, and then we'd find a good place to trot or canter or sometimes have a wild gallop. Shelby never enjoyed that as much as I did. She always likes to feel in control—and it was true that every once in a while John would get excited and try to take the bit in his mouth and bolt, and I'd have to put a burst of speed on Tracker to head John off.

Things like that didn't happen very often, though, and I thought Shelby was having as much fun as I was. I was glad to see she'd lost some of her prissy riding-school manners. Maybe she was beginning to realize that this was what horses were *for*—to go places and see things, to feel free, the horses and the riders both. Keeping them cooped up in a stable, always behind fences, making them go through a lot of fancy maneuvers just to make their riders look good, was cruel and unnatural. (I've changed my mind about this a bit now that I've seen what Tracker can do. But it's still not my kind of riding.)

That next winter was a mild one, and we rode whenever we could, after school and on weekends. I loved looking out at the barn on frosty mornings and seeing the two heads, the brown and the gray, looking out at me, waiting for their breakfast and wondering if

I was going to make something happen that day. Usually I'd help Shelby with the evening feed and grooming, which we made last longer than we really needed to, in spite of the cold—leaning up against our horses' flanks to feel their warmth, smelling the good summery smells of manure and hay.

In the spring, whenever I wasn't busy with Pony Club, we went back to taking our long rides together. I hardly noticed when one of the dirt roads was paved over, and some city people bought the Vincents' house and wouldn't let us use their driveway as a shortcut because there might be droppings or a petunia might get stepped on. There were still plenty of places to ride.

Then there was the Pony Club rally, which as I say was no big deal, except that people began taking notice of Tracker. Pam, for one. She'd become part-owner of the riding academy, and it wasn't so run-down and dinky any more. In fact, they'd added a new stable block and put in a proper dressage ring and replaced all the old splintery fences with gleaming white rails. A lot of the new people moving into the area wanted their kids to have riding lessons, it seemed. Anyway, Pam told my parents that even if I was quitting Pony Club it would be a shame not to go on with the jumping I'd been learning, especially when I had a good horse like Tracker. She offered to come help us set up some jumps in the front field, and said she'd find time to give me a lesson now and then. She even gave us a special rate.

And that's when Shelby started riding Tracker—really riding him, I mean—for the first time.

5

Larry has been listening patiently to all this, nodding from time to time, smiling a little when I describe those long, carefree rides we used to take. I know he understands that part—about wanting to feel free, not boxed in by fences or rules or whatever. It's the way he tries to live himself. But now, as I pause, staring into the fire and hugging my knees up under my chin—the room hasn't gotten much warmer—he says sharply, "She moved in on your lessons, you mean?"

"No. Not exactly. It was just—well, anyone could see how much Shelby wanted to try jumping herself.

Like I said, she used to be bored when I had my lessons on Max, but with Tracker it was different. She was always there, watching. Really watching, I mean, as if she was trying to memorize the whole deal, including all the things I did wrong. Shelby says you can learn a lot from other people's mistakes."

Larry mutters something that sounds like "She would," but when I look at him he just shakes his head and says, "Go on."

"Well, so one day Pam asked her if she'd like to have a try, and of course Shelby said yes. She was nervous, but it was amazing how much she'd learned just from watching. Pam said she really ought to be having lessons, too, and maybe mine could be cut down from an hour to a half-hour, now that I'd learned the basics, and Shelby could have the other half-hour. That was fine with me. To tell the truth, a whole hour seemed like a lot of time to spend just going over the same old jumps. I mean, there didn't seem to be all that much *to* it, and Tracker knew what to do anyway. Pam would raise the jumps another notch and Tracker would just go sailing over them. All I had to do was stay on and not interfere, if you know what I mean. Of course, Pam was always yelling at me for being sloppy—or looking sloppy, I guess that was really the point—but I couldn't see why it mattered, as long as Tracker jumped clean."

"But I bet Shelby could," Larry says. "I bet she

45

did every single thing Pam told her to do. If Pam said, don't blink, Shelby would never, ever blink again. Right?"

Again his tone disturbs me. "Well, I told you, Shelby's a perfectionist, she likes to get things right. Not like me. And if you could see her riding Tracker—well, it's really beautiful. I admit I didn't understand at first. In fact, I guess I was a little jealous when Pam started getting so interested in Shelby. But after Shelby'd had a couple of lessons I began to see what Pam meant. It's a kind of picture the horse and rider make together . . . and there's this feeling of perfect balance and control. . . ." My voice trails away. I can't really explain what I mean, partly, I guess, because the whole idea is something I still resist.

"Beautiful, maybe," Larry says, "but artificial. Unnatural. And then you add the element of competition. . . ." He sighs, closing his eyes. The flames snap in the fireplace, and the wind roars in the chimney and drives the rain against the tall windows. "So then I suppose the next logical step is that Shelby borrows your horse to ride in a show?"

"No. I mean, she rode one of Pam's horses in her first few shows. Anyway, that wasn't till last spring, a year ago. The really important time was the summer before, the time I'm talking about, when Shelby was learning to jump and Mr. Peterson found out about it."

46

I look anxiously at Larry, worrying that I'm boring him with all this. But he straightens up, saying intently, "Peterson? Big blond guy who always wears a checked shirt? He's on the Planning Commission? Works down at Kingsley and Rowe?"

I nod. "That's him. Shelby's father."

Larry grimaces. "I've had a few run-ins with him. I'm not exactly one of his favorite citizens around here, in case you didn't know. . . . Well, never mind that. How do you mean, he found out?"

"Well . . . at first Shelby didn't say anything to her parents about the jumping. She was afraid they wouldn't like it, even though she always wore her hard hat and there was always a teacher right there and everything. She did a lot of extra baby-sitting to earn the money for the lessons, and—well, they just didn't know anything about it. I told her it was wrong, but she said it wasn't really lying because they'd never asked her about it. Boy, was Pam mad when she found out! In fact I don't know who was madder, Pam or Mr. Peterson."

I grin, remembering that morning—Pam, who's small and wiry and a lot tougher than she looks, glaring at Shelby; and Mr. Peterson (who, as Larry says, is a big man, and probably even tougher than he looks) not knowing who to yell at louder, Shelby or Pam. Not that it was so funny at the time. It happened to be Shelby's half of the lesson, and none of us saw him coming. His car wouldn't start, and he was walking up the hill to borrow Dad's jump cables. He was already late for work and not exactly in a great mood. And then what does he see but his precious youngest daughter riding a horse—and not even her own horse—straight at a three-and-a-half foot jump, looking about to break her neck. Well, you can imagine.

But finally, after Pam had finished telling Shelby off, she made Mr. Peterson calm down long enough to watch Shelby take Tracker once around the course. Shelby had been standing white-faced and silent beside Tracker, clutching his bridle; but when Pam gave one of her quick okay-do-your-stuff nods, Shelby swung back up into the saddle and touched his flanks, and they moved off toward the first jump. It was a beautiful day in early September, and I remember how the red sumac and the goldenrod, growing tall at the edge of the field, made a kind of frame against the blue sky for the arching figure of the gray horse and the girl leaning forward along his neck.

Mr. Peterson didn't say anything, but I could tell he was impressed in spite of himself. I was impressed too, because if it had been me I probably would have fallen off, or lost my stirrups, or just started bawling. But Shelby just did everything the way she'd been taught, and you never would have guessed how much she was shaking inside. Usually when Mr. Peterson loses his temper everyone in that family just lies down and dies.

"Four girls," I explain to Larry. "Mom says his problem is that he always wanted a son. Maybe she's right, because—well, it's like he never paid much attention to them as long as they looked nice and behaved themselves. Shelby's always been his favorite, because of being the youngest and the prettiest, but even with her . . . I don't know, you never felt he was really *interested*, the way he would have been with a boy. He used to be a football player, in fact he played pro football for a while, only he had a bad injury—his back, I think—and had to quit. I guess if he'd had sons he would have done sports and things with them, but with only girls . . . well, he never even played catch with them, or put up a basketball net, or any of the other stuff my father did with me—stuff that lots of fathers do with their daughters."

"Not only a jock," Larry remarks, "but a chauvinist besides. I think I begin to understand Shelby a little better."

"He's not really that bad," I protest. "I mean, maybe he is a heavy father, but at least he's fair. And anyway, Mrs. Peterson can usually kid him out of his bad moods. . . . Besides, you can't call him a chauvinist any more, not with the way he's been encouraging Shelby ever since that day. Poor Shelby, she thought he was going to say she could never ride again." I smile and shake my head, remembering. "Instead of which he starts asking Pam lots of questions, he's listening and nodding, not even looking at Shelby, and before you know it he's making a deal for more lessons over at the academy and asking about an indoor ring where she can work out over the winter. It was as if he made up his mind right then and there that Shelby was going to be the best, even if he'd practically never heard of show riding before then."

"Expensive," Larry says, raising his eyebrows; and I nod, thinking of how Molly and Donna have jobs after school now, and how Karen only got to have two bridesmaids instead of the four she wanted, and the reception at home instead of at the Cloverleaf Inn. But as my father said after reading an article about some teenage ice skater or tennis player, having a talented athlete in the family means that everyone has to make sacrifices.

"Well, I just hope you've put a fair price on Tracker," Larry says—and lets the words hang between us, heavy in the silence.

I bow my head. I can feel him watching me, waiting. "If only I had some place to ride him," I say at last, in a muffled voice. "But there are hardly any left."

"Hardly any of what left?" Rita is barefoot, like Larry, and I didn't hear her come into the room. She's carrying a couple of steaming mugs, which she hands to Larry and me. When I hesitate, she says, "No, that's for you, Kate. I'm fasting. I just thought I'd take a break and come say hello."

Larry teases Rita about her fasting, saying it's just another word for a crash diet. I guess she is a bit overweight, though it's hard to tell, what with the clothes she wears—long sack dresses that she weaves herself. She has springy dark hair and rosy cheeks (rosier than usual today, it must be really cold up in the tower room where she has her loom) and a calm, smiling gaze that reminds me a little of my mother's.

She settles herself on one of the windowseats, tucking one foot up under her, and repeats her question. Larry explains briefly, and Rita sighs. "I can imagine. The way this town has been built up in the few years we've been here . . . it's really changed a lot, the people especially. All these corporation types and their families. Next thing you know they'll be building a country club." She says it as if it's a dirty word, and Larry grins. "We've been thinking of moving on, but I don't know. This house is so perfect for us, and wherever we went the same thing would probably happen all over again, the way these so-called light industries seem to be taking over the countryside."

I take a cautious sip from my mug—it's green herbal tea with honey in it, which I personally find yucky, but today the warmth feels good—and think that at least the new people don't seem to object to things like mixed-up households and peculiar clothes the way the old-timers do. Also that Rita has been selling a lot more of her expensive table mats and wall hangings since all the new money came to town.

Rita says, "But out where you are, Kate, there must be *some* open country left."

I shake my head. "Not too much. Not like it used to be. I mean, when my parents first moved here, before I was born, it was really country—mostly farms, and just a few houses down by Stewart's Market." She looks blank, so I explain, "Where the Millbrook Mall is now. Dad says he was always having to apologize for only owning ten acres and being just a summer farmer—you know, just raising a few pigs and chickens. He doesn't even have time for that any more, he has to work so hard just to make enough money to pay the taxes on the land. Which is sort of crazy, when you think about it."

Larry smiles wryly. "And now he's one of the big landowners. . . . But seriously, Kate, there must still be places you can take Tracker for a good workout. I mean, that's the real problem, isn't it? That you can't keep Tracker unless you can exercise him."

"Well, all horses need exercise just to stay healthy. But some need more than others, and Tracker—"

"And Tracker's a good horse," Larry finishes for me. I nod unhappily. "So okay, let's do a little research on this thing." Suddenly he's full of energy, he jumps to his feet and goes into the front hall, where I can hear him rummaging around in the drawer of the big table there. "I've got a good map here somewhere," he mutters.

Rita smiles at me. "Nothing Larry likes better than a challenge," she says. "You wouldn't think it to look at him, but"—she shrugs—"I guess it's built in. Comes with the upbringing."

"Well, it's nice of him to want to help," I say, setting my mug down carefully on the floor and hoping Rita won't notice it's still half full. "But I've tried all kinds of places, and— See, it isn't so much finding a place to ride as it is *getting* there. There used to be lots of shortcuts you could take, but now it's all highways and fences and people's yards, and if you have to hack Tracker too far, he . . . well, he gets nervous about it."

What I haven't admitted to Larry, and what I don't dare tell my parents or Shelby—Shelby least of all— is that Tracker isn't just spooky on the roads these days, he's on the verge of panic a lot of the time. Sometimes it's all I can do to control him. In spite of my brave words to Mom, I hardly ever take him to Munson's Woods any more because there's a new bridge you have to cross to get there, a big concrete thing with reflectors along the sides and weird-looking lights on tall poles. Tracker didn't like the old blacktop bridge much either, but at least you didn't have to drag him across it, with him snorting and sweating and rolling his eyes. It's also a long hack to the fields beyond the elementary school, with lots of traffic. Anyway those fields are being used for Little League games now. The power line is okay, but you can't do much except walk along it because the ground is so broken and rough.

As for Bayberry Lane—well, it's still a dirt road all right, but the last time I rode there someone was digging a new well, and just the sound of the machine was enough for Tracker, before he even saw it. He took off, really bolted with me for the first time since the summer I got him and was still learning to control him. It was lucky that we *were* on a dirt road and that there wasn't any traffic.

Larry comes back with a battered large-scale map of the township, and spreads it out on the floor. I can see right away that it isn't up-to-date—well, the way things are, you'd practically have to have a map made last week for it to be really up-to-date—but I hunker down beside him, and after a moment Rita comes over to join us.

"Now how about this," Larry says, tracing a route with his finger—it shows just a couple of X's for houses, but I happen to know there's also a big plant nursery there now—"or this—"

"Hey, what about all this space out here?" Rita plunks a callused thumb down on the northeast corner of the map, which shows only a few roads and hardly any X's. It's a part of the township we rarely even drive through because it's not on the way to anywhere. A long way from home, but still. . . .

I sit back on my heels, considering. At least it's a place I haven't tried. Maybe Larry's right, I think, with a little spurt of hope. Maybe I've been giving up too soon.

Together we study the map.

6

The next day, Thursday, Shelby comes up after school to give Tracker his workout, as planned. It's a cloudy afternoon, but warm and sticky, and when I see her walking back from the barn I call to her to come have some lemonade with me on the front porch. She stops in the kitchen first to wash the sweat and grime from her hands and face, and then comes out onto the porch and flops down beside me on the old glider swing, which creaks loudly in protest.

"Thanks," she says, taking a long swallow from the glass I hand her. "He really went good today, in spite of all the mud. In fact I think he almost does better when the ground is tacky. Do you know what the forecast is for the weekend by any chance?"

I shake my head. Shelby gives me a quick glance and sees that I don't want to talk about the show. She looks down at her mud-splattered breeches and grimaces. "Boy, am I a mess. There's a big puddle on the far side of the corner jump, and every time we went over it, *whoosh*. Almost like a real water jump, come to think of it," she adds with a grin.

I've been feeling so much better after my talk with Larry that I've forgotten I haven't yet told Shelby about how the front field's being sold. I tell her now. For a moment we are both silent, gazing out at the familiar contours of the field across the road, with its matchstick pattern of angled white gates, and at the gentle downward slope of the hills beyond, defined by clumps of trees whose new leaves are a vivid lime-green on this gray afternoon.

"Well, I guess it was bound to happen, sooner or later," Shelby says at last.

"I guess."

"But maybe they won't start building for a while. I mean, we can still go on riding there for now, can't we?"

"As far as I know," I say, passing over the "we." "At least they haven't put up a No Trespassing sign, or anything. Yet."

But when they do . . . Shelby knows what this will mean as well as I do, to both of us; but she doesn't say anything, keeping to our pact. Instead she takes another swallow of lemonade and says, still staring at the field, "I wonder what kind of houses they'll build there."

"Oh—" I shrug. "Probably more of those big, white boxes. The land's pretty expensive, so they won't be dinky little houses. Just a lot of windows looking at our windows."

"Well, the good view will be at the back," Shelby says, trying to comfort me. "Maybe they won't have too many windows in front. Or maybe they'll even put up some of those, you know, contemporary deals, the kind where everything's built at an angle. Like the new houses down along Three Mile Road. I think they're neat-looking, don't you?"

"In a weird kind of way. But at least they've got trees around them. A house like that would look ridiculous up here. And anyway, can you imagine wanting to live in one of those?"

"Sure. In fact, that's just the kind of house I'd like to have someday."

"Oh, Shelby! I'd rather live in one of the boxes, if I had to choose."

"Oh, Kate!" she mimicks me. "You're such a— what's the word?—a conservative. Poor old Taurus. Now if you'd been born an Aries, like me . . ."

58

She shakes her head pityingly, and we both grin. It's a familiar joke between us. "I bet you really would've been happier living back in the nineteenth century, wouldn't you?"

"Except for the clothes," I agree, stretching out my legs in their comfortable worn jeans and wiggling my bare toes.

"Speaking of houses"—Shelby gives the swing a push with one foot, and it creaks again—"where did you go after school yesterday? The Zoo?"

"I wish you wouldn't call it that," I say sharply. "Just because your parents—"

"Okay, okay." She raises an arm in front of her face, pretending to fend me off. "I just don't understand what the big attraction is. I mean, unless you have a thing for what's-his-name, Larry." She makes a face. "Of course I've only seen him from a distance, but still . . ."

"Come off it, Shelby." I know she's just teasing, but still I feel a flare of anger. "He's a really nice guy. I just like to talk to him, that's all. You'd like him too if you got to know him."

She considers this for a moment, then shakes her head definitely. "No, I wouldn't. And he wouldn't like me either, I bet."

"If you mean because of your dad—"

"Partly that, but partly . . . Oh, I don't know, I just can't understand anyone wanting to live like that.

59

I don't mean just the house, I mean not having any ambition—not caring about anything, or wanting to make something out of your life."

"Larry cares about lots of things," I object.

"Oh, Kate, you know what I mean."

I shrug. "Well, anyway, that still doesn't mean Larry wouldn't like *you*," I say, but without much conviction.

Actually it's crossed my mind to take Shelby over to Larry's house with me someday, if only to show Larry she isn't the kind of hard, ruthless character he seems to be imagining. But when I try to picture Shelby in that big, bare living room, wrinkling her nose at the cobwebs and the dust and the jelly jar full of dead wildflowers on the mantlepiece, I see that it wouldn't work. Not that she would—wrinkle her nose, I mean. But the effect would be the same. Whenever Shelby feels uncomfortable or out of place she tends to put on her preppiest manner, very cool and superior. And then if Larry started needling her . . . if he brought up the subject of Tracker, which he probably would . . .

Tess has been lying on the cool stone slab at the bottom of the porch steps. Now she raises her head, sniffs, and begins to growl. There's a crawlway under the porch, where Shelby and I used to play when we were little. Something must be under there—a squirrel, maybe, or a chipmunk. Not a skunk, I hope and pray.

"Hush, Tess," I say. But she gets stiffly to her feet and begins barking in that high, excited way collies do. At the same time her tail is waving.

"Oh, well, I'd better go see what it is," I say resignedly, leaving the swing. At the bottom of the steps I hunker down, trying to see into the crawlway. After a moment I make out a familiar, comical face—bright eyes in a black mask, a sharp pointed nose. "It's Budge," I call to Shelby. "He must have broken his chain again. Here, Budgie, it's okay—come on out, Tess won't hurt you."

But the raccoon is wary of the dog, and Shelby has to shut Tess in the house before Budge will leave the crawlway and come to me with his funny, sidling walk.

"Miss Emory is probably having a fit," I say, stroking Budge's coarse gray coat. "Good Budgie, give me your paw, that's right." I shake one of his front paws, which is really more like a small black hand, and smile over my shoulder at Shelby. Shaking hands is one of the tricks Miss Emory taught him. She lives down beyond our pond in a cottage right on the road, and we've all gotten used to seeing her out walking her three raccoons on leashes, just like dogs.

I notice that Budge still has his collar on, so I say

61

to Shelby, "Here, you hold him for a minute while I go get a leash."

Shelby makes a face, but does as I ask. When I come out of the house again she gladly turns Budge back over to me. "Why anyone would want a raccoon for a pet. . . ." She shakes her head.

"Oh, Shelby, I think they're cute. And smart too. Much smarter than most dogs."

"But they're wild animals. Or they're supposed to be. You're the one who's always wanting things to be free, not tied up or penned in." She grins suddenly. "Remember the baby squirrel we found back of my house and took care of until it was ready to be on its own? And then how it wouldn't leave? No matter how far we took it into the woods, it kept coming back and begging for food. Every time my mother opened the back door, there was that same darned squirrel."

"Until finally we got Billy Tucker to take it," I agree. "We figured since he already had a boa constrictor and a spider collection, his parents probably wouldn't mind a nice normal pet like a tame squirrel."

We both laugh; but Shelby's expression changes as she watches me clip the leash to the raccoon's collar. "But this—I don't know, it's just not *natural*, that's all."

"Good boy, Budge. . . . I know, and I used to feel that way too, but now—well, at least they're safe with

Miss Emory. You know what happens to raccoons around here these days, people trap them, and even shoot them, just because they get into the garbage."

"They can make an awful mess," Shelby says.

"Sure, but if people covered their garbage cans like they're supposed to do . . . I mean, when you live in the country raccoons are just something you have to expect and plan for. . . ." My voice trails off; suddenly I remember that one of the people who shoots raccoons is Shelby's father. Two raccoons, anyway— a female and her cub, last summer. Shelby was pretty upset about it at the time. She bites her lip and looks away.

I brought out one of Tess's dog biscuits for Budge. I give it to him now. He holds it between his black hands for a moment, examining it carefully, then sits back on his haunches and begins to devour it with his sharp teeth.

Shelby's face softens as she watches him. In an off-hand tone, she says, "Well, I guess maybe I could walk him home. I should be going anyhow, and it's on my way if I take the shortcut." Down our lower lawn and past the pond, she means. "Miss Emory may not be living there much longer anyway, did you know?" she adds, as I hand her the leash.

"No," I say, startled. Miss Emory taught school for years—Shelby and I both had her in fourth grade— and even though she retired a couple of years ago I can't imagine her living anywhere but in her cottage, with its tidy flowerbeds and the climbing yellow rose over the front door.

"They're trying to buy her out," Shelby explains. "The people who're doing the new development in the woods behind. Something about a right of way. Well, I don't really know much about it, but my dad says she's crazy not to sell, at the price they're offering. She says she won't move because of the raccoons, but Dad thinks she's just trying to jack the price up even higher."

We both look down at Budge, who's finished his dog biscuit and is making that funny washing motion of his front paws that raccoons sometimes do. "Well, I can understand about the raccoons," I say slowly. "I mean, they're used to that one place, and Miss Emory can let them run free there, for a couple of hours at a time anyway. Somewhere else—well, it probably wouldn't be the same."

"If she could even find a place," Shelby says practically. "A lot of people might not want raccoons for neighbors." She yawns suddenly. "Oh wow, I'm beat, and I still have a ton of homework to do. Come on, Budge, let's get going." She gives the leash a twitch, and Budge shifts obediently onto all fours.

"Don't forget to bring the leash back," I call, as they move away.

"Nope. See you tomorrow."

They make a funny picture going down the lawn—Shelby, with her bright hair, sauntering along in her riding clothes, the fat raccoon waddling at her heels. Suddenly the lump is back in my throat. Poor Miss Emory, I think. From my father I know something about the kinds of pressures the big developers can bring to bear on someone like Miss Emory, who lives alone and doesn't have any money or influence to fight them with. If she doesn't hold out much longer it won't be just because of the price, whatever Shelby's father may think. Or pretend to think. As Larry pointed out, Mr. Peterson is on the Planning Commission.

Poor Miss Emory. Poor me. I look once more at the field across the way before I pick up the pitcher and glasses and go inside. No, *dumb* me, I correct myself in self-disgust—wasting time feeling sorry for myself when I could have been out exploring. Miss Emory may not have much of a chance, but I do. Larry's map says I do.

The next day after school I get on my bike and head northeast along a winding blacktop road. I've never ridden Tracker far in this direction, partly because it's so hilly, partly because the first open land you come to all seems to belong to one big estate, with a high brick wall running alongside the house and grounds and the rest of it securely fenced.

Today I pedal on past the estate—catching a glimpse of some sleek Herefords grazing in a meadow, but no horses—toward the patch of open countryside shown on the map. If there does turn out to be good riding ahead, it will be quite a distance to hack. But at least there's hardly any traffic, and nothing threatening beside the road that I can see. On a road like this, I think, maybe I could get Tracker to relax again. And right here, where the land levels out for a bit, there's even a nice wide stretch of gravel shoulder where we could trot or canter. . . .

I come to a fork, where the map says to bear left. As I do I notice a small makeshift sign pointing in that direction. "Apple Ridge," it says. I've never heard of Apple Ridge, and it's not on the map. A farm maybe, or more likely the name of a house. The new people are always giving fancy names to their houses, and when they have a party they sometimes put up signs like these for their friends and forget to take them down afterwards.

The road begins to climb again, and pretty soon I'm too breathless to think about anything except getting to the top of the next hill. When I do, I find out what Apple Ridge is, or will be when it's finished—a brand-new golf course. From here I can see the fairways beginning to take shape, looping back and forth across a gentle valley which must once have been mostly orchards. They've left a lot of the old apple trees dotted around, but they've adding wind-breaks of evergreens and poplars. On the opposite hillside I can see a long low building that must be the clubhouse. There are patches of emerald green below it, and what looks like a sand truck parked by a dazzling white bunker. They're already finishing the first few holes.

I suppose it will be a beautiful golf course when it's done, if you happen to like golf courses.

I turn my bike around. At least it will be downhill most of the way home. And with any luck Pam and Shelby will already have come and gone with the van, taking Tracker-the-good-horse with them.

7

We've just finished dinner on Sunday night when we hear Tess barking outside and look out to see the van pulling into the driveway. All weekend long I've been missing Tracker—it's the longest he's ever been gone—but I keep myself from rushing out to the barn. Instead I take my plate over to the sink and turn on the hot water. It's my night for doing the dishes. I can hear John whinnying gladly out in the paddock as the van eases along the track. He was so restless this morning that I finally gave in and took him for a long ride. The well digger was still thumping away on Bayberry Lane—the people there must be getting really desperate for water—but John barely glanced at it as we went by. You can ride John anywhere, you could probably even ride him alongside the interstate highway without his batting an eye.

"Never mind about the dishes, Kate," my mother says. "You go on out if you want to."

I put a glass carefully in the dishwasher. "They don't need me to help unload him. I'll go out later."

After they've left, I mean, when I can say my own special hello to Tracker and be alone with him. Alone except for John anyway.

Dad says, "Don't you want to find out how they did?"

"Not particularly."

"Kate—" I can feel that he's about to lecture me on what he'll call my lack of elementary good manners. It's one thing he's big on. He says just going through the motions is good for the soul. But I think that if having good manners means acting the opposite of the way you feel, it's not much different from telling a lie.

Anyway, Mom must have shaken her head at him because he doesn't say anything more. I hear him push back his chair, and then the scrape of one of the wooden matches he uses to light his pipe against the matchbox. "Well," he says, "back to the salt mines"—meaning the den he uses as an office—and

69

leaves the kitchen, trailing a faint aroma of pipe smoke. I'm glad to be spared the lecture, but I hate this, the way my parents have taken to acting so careful around me, as if I was sick or something.

Maybe I am. I guess a lot of people would say it's sick to care so much about anything, especially a dumb animal, a horse who doesn't even love you back the way you love him and who will forget all about you in a few months, once he's with new people and smells and sounds, and other horses. . . .

I wonder how long it will take John to forget Tracker.

Mom says, "Well, I think I'll just go out and say hello." She takes her old denim jacket from the hook by the back door and goes out, calling over her shoulder, "Oh, Kate, you should see the sunset! It's going to be a beautiful day tomorrow."

The kitchen faces east, so all you can see of the sunset from here is the afterglow. But I don't even look out the window. Instead I scrub the frying pan and think about John, who's easier to think about than Tracker, even though he's a problem, too. When the Petersons made their offer for Tracker they said they'd throw in John, if I wanted him. If not, they'd find another home for him, and pay that much more for Tracker. (When Mr. Peterson started mentioning prices Dad stopped him, saying there'd be time enough to talk about that when I made up my mind, and anyway, the money wasn't important, we'd settle for what we paid for Tracker in the first place.)

I guess in a way John is really more my horse now than he is Shelby's. At least, I'm the only one who rides him. In fact I even find myself feeling guilty about not riding him more, which is really dumb, because he's still Shelby's responsibility, after all. But although she goes on feeding and grooming him automatically I don't think she ever really gives him a thought. She's outgrown him, the way I outgrew Max, and that's that. To be fair, I didn't think much about Max either, not after I got Tracker. But then, Max wasn't still around, looking at me mournfully, grateful for a passing word or a casual pat on the neck.

If I sell Tracker and Shelby takes him away I think I'd just as soon look at empty stalls, both of them. Besides, John would be lonely, whether it was Tracker he was missing or (after a while) just the company of another horse. He'd be better off at someplace like a riding stable. He's not so young any more, and his mouth is like cement, but he'd be okay for beginners. Maybe Pam would even take him for the academy. If only he wasn't so tall. Pam prefers ponies for beginners, even if they're bratty (the ponies, I mean, not the kids). She says it reassures the parents.

I'm sponging off the counters and starting to set the table for breakfast when the back door opens and Shelby and Pam come in, followed by Mom and Mrs.

Peterson, who's saying, "Oh, boy, lead me to that cup of coffee and make it strong! I need something to help glue my bones back together. I came back in the van," she explains to me, unnecessarily. "At least I got to test all my new gold inlays that I'm probably going to be in hock for to Dr. Davies for the next twenty years."

If Mrs. Peterson were a character in a play the directions would say something like *Enter talking a mile a minute.* And it's not only her mouth, the rest of her is never still either. While Mom gets out mugs and milk and sugar Mrs. Peterson stands chatting to her at the counter, drumming her manicured fingernails on the formica, tapping the toe of one foot in its high-heeled sandal. She's wearing a silky green tunic-and-skirt outfit with a fancy belt—the latest thing, no doubt, although probably not for horse shows. I figure whatever it costs to keep Shelby in horses and equipment and riding habits and entrance fees, the one thing that won't be cut from the budget is Mrs. Peterson's clothes.

(Well, to be fair, she's worked at a lot of boring jobs—her description—just to earn money for things like clothes and hairdos. Right now she's working at a big furniture showroom where she says she walks at least five miles a day around all the sofas and chairs, and never gets to sit down.)

Pam is using the phone to call her partner, checking

on the teaching schedule for tomorrow. Shelby slumps down at the table. She looks tired, and there's a smudge on the narrow white collar of her striped stock shirt. She hasn't changed, except to trade her boots for a pair of old suede moccasins.

"No, just fourth in the Good Hands, nothing in the jumping," Pam is saying into the phone, standing with one fist cocked on her hip. Even in a dusty work shirt and jeans, at the end of a long day, Pam crackles with energy. "I nearly died when I saw who was judging—old Bellmeister, you know, he still thinks he's back in the U.S. Cavalry. . . ."

"Tracker's fine," Shelby tells me wearily, knowing that's what I want to hear first. "In fact, he did great. I was the one who goofed."

Mrs. Peterson breaks off her conversation with my mother to say, "Now, Shelby, you know that just isn't true. You were up against a lot of stiff competition, that's all. Some of the best young riders in the East," she explains to Mom and me—overnight Mrs. P. has become an authority on horse shows—"to say nothing of the horses. Oh, you should have seen them, Kate, there were some real beauties. What was the name of that gorgeous chestnut, the one that took first in the Open Jumper?"

"Cinnamon King," Pam supplies, hanging up the phone and accepting a cup of coffee from Mom. She sits down across from Shelby and stirs it thoughtfully.

"I liked that bay mare too, Felicity. Remember, in the Novice Equitation?" Shelby nods. I can tell all she wants to do is get home to bed where she can finally let herself cry a little without anyone hearing. "She's still green," Pam continues, "but a few years from now . . . Well, it's always a good idea to keep an eye open for the future."

At first I assume Pam is thinking about her own string of horses—right now she has a couple of hunters and an Arabian pleasure mare—or of the stock she's building up at the academy. Then I realize she's thinking about Shelby.

Of course. If Shelby goes on with this thing, if she's really serious about show riding, sooner or later she'll need another horse—a better horse than Tracker. And Tracker will be discarded, the way John has been, and Max. He will be sold to someone else, some other girl who needs an intermediate horse for a year or so, a horse that can teach her something and win some ribbons; and then, after he's served his purpose, he'll be passed on again. I can see the ad in the paper: "Gray gelding, 15.2 hands, good jumper, has shown successfully." And I'll never even know those other people. I'll never even know where Tracker is.

Something in me seems to crumple up. I let myself down slowly into a chair, Dad's chair at the end of the table. I realize I'm still holding the sponge. It's

74

a bright orange sponge, too bright—a loud, fake color against the honest wood color of the table. There are a few flakes of pipe tobacco I missed when I wiped the table before. I brush them off and then sit squeezing the sponge as hard as I can in my right hand, watching my knuckles go white and shiny.

Mom is putting the milk back in the fridge. She turns and looks at me gravely. Has she understood this about Tracker all along? I feel an unreasonable flicker of anger at her, and at myself for being so dumb, or maybe for just not seeing what I didn't want to see. Then Mrs. Peterson speaks, and at her words the crumpled thing inside me flares back into life, her voice rasping at me like one of my father's kitchen matches.

"You'll be letting us know soon, won't you, Katie?" (I hate being called Katie.) "About Tracker, I mean. Because we do want to get this thing settled, and there's just a chance that Janet Crowley might let us have that nice Connemara of hers. He's smaller than Tracker, of course, but a good jumper. She's off to college in the fall and she was going to wait until then to sell him, but if we made a good offer. . . ." I don't know what my face looks like, but Mrs. Peterson must have noticed something because she pats my shoulder and adds hastily, "You've been wonderful, dear, letting us borrow Tracker all this time, but

I guess you realize it's kind of an awkward situation for Shelby, not really having a horse she can call her own—"

"It's awkward for Kate, too," Shelby interrupts in her clear voice. She looks at me directly, her eyes very blue and steady. "Tracker is still my first choice," she says.

Am I supposed to be grateful to her for saying that? I don't know. "Mine too," I say, just as clearly. For a moment, our glances hold. Then suddenly we are grinning wryly at each other.

Shelby at least understands something of what I'm feeling. But Pam, as usual, is all business. She says decisively, "Tracker is perfect for Shelby at this point. Janet's Connemara is a good pony, but all he's ever done is Pony Clubbing and a few local shows. Speaking of which—" She runs a hand through her short dark hair and turns to me, squinting a little in the way she does when she's figuring out schedules and plans. "The Gainesville show is coming up three weeks from now. A few years ago it didn't amount to much, but they've built it up into a fairly good event. Shelby ought to do quite well, I think, especially in the jumping. But if she's going to be riding a new horse obviously she'll need some time to work with him. Do you think you could decide about Tracker by next weekend, Kate? It's really kind of important."

They are all looking at me—Mrs. Peterson's mascaraed blue eyes, paler than Shelby's, Mom's soft dark gaze, Pam's cool hazel stare. Or not all of them: Shelby is staring down at the table, biting her lip. I take a deep breath and relax my grip on the stupid sponge, which I find I am still squeezing. "I guess so," I say at last. "I guess it's hard on everybody, going on like this. Maybe on Tracker, too. He doesn't know from one day to the next whether he's supposed to be a show horse or—or just an overgrown backyard pet."

Even Pam smiles a little at this, and I see them all relax. Perversely, my anger burns up bright again. They're so sure, I think. They think they've got me boxed in, with no place to go. But maybe they're wrong. And I've still got a week to find out.

Wednesday is the last day of school, a half-day—we get out at noon. On Wednesday, Tracker and I will take Millbrook Road as far as the old firehouse, and then we'll try the new shortcut to the quarry I think I may have found on Larry's map.

I dump my last-day-of-school gear on the kitchen table—gym shorts, a lot of messy junk from my locker, and of course my report card, which is better than I expected—and pick up the note Mom has left for me. "Sorry not to be on hand to help celebrate, but got invited over to the Lehrmans' for a swim, and couldn't resist. Chops may be defrosted by now, if so please put in fridge. See you later. LOVE—"

Mom always signs her notes that way, just LOVE and a big dash. I smile to myself and inspect the package of veal chops before I forget. They've already thawed under their plastic wrapping—not surprising, considering the weather. It's a hot, thundery day, overcast and very humid. Tess didn't come bounding down the driveway to greet me, the way she usually does, but only waved her tail apologetically at me from underneath the big forsythia bush. For a moment I think longingly of the Lehrmans' pool—well, it isn't a pool really, just a dammed-up place in the river, but the water will still be cold and clear this early in the year—and tell myself it's a crazy kind of day to go riding.

At least thunder doesn't bother Tracker particularly. Natural things mostly don't. A flurry of birds in the undergrowth, a woodchuck popping out of its burrow, a dog nosing at his heels—he might startle a little, but usually he takes such things in his stride. He'd never develop a rabbit phobia, like silly old John. It's just the man-made things that scare him. I think this is partly because of where he was raised, upstate. The people who owned him were quite rich, I guess. They lived in New York City, and this was just their summer place—a big house and lots of land, including some woods where they had bridle trails. I don't think Tracker was ever ridden much on the roads, and even if he was, they were quiet country roads, just lanes really, with hardly any traffic. I'm sure he never met up with a motorcycle before he came here, let alone a garbage truck or a moving van or a bulldozer. Farm machinery was the only kind that didn't bother him, at least to begin with. Now he even gets nervous about tractors, and he's been seeing them all his life.

On the bus I told Shelby I was going to ride Tracker today, and when she said, "Where?" I pretended I couldn't hear her, or anyway couldn't answer, because of all the racket the kids were making, yelling and singing. When the driver let her out at the bottom of the hill, she called, "Tomorrow morning, okay?" and I nodded.

Maybe tomorrow morning I won't mind watching her work with Tracker in the front field. Maybe by tomorrow Tracker and I will have a place of our own to go.

And if there's one place there's bound to be another. In fact, I think hopefully, if Tracker and I could just have a few good rides together I'd be able to start calming him down again. He'd trust me instead of fighting me, and we could go back to places like Munson's Woods and Bayberry Lane, and maybe even go as far as the state park on the other side of town, where there are some real trails. . . .

I had lunch at eleven o'clock at school—of all the weird times to have lunch—but I get a carton of strawberry yogurt from the fridge and spoon it up slowly while I study the map. Not that I trust the map particularly, but it still shows the area around the quarry the way it used to be, no new roads leading into it from the state highway below, only dotted lines for the old trucking road at one end and Mr. Schuller's driveway at the other, with the X that means "residence" on the map.

Anyway, I decide, we'd know if Mr. Schuller had died or moved away because he's sort of a famous character around here. His "residence" is just a shack that he built in the woods when he came here after World War II. Some people say he's an ex-Nazi, some say he was in a concentration camp. Either way, it seems that all he's ever wanted was to be left alone. He's not a hermit exactly—you see him driving around town in his little pickup truck, and he always nods and is very polite—but he never says more than a few sentences to anyone, as if he only knew that much English. Dad says his English is actually quite good. Dad knows because he helped draw up the agreement that Mr. Schuller made with the gravel company some years ago.

Everyone was surprised that Mr. Schuller would want quarrying going on on his property, and they waited to see what he would do with the money. But nothing changed. He went on living in his little shack, and when the land was quarried out and the last truck had left he put a bar across the track and nailed a No Trespassing sign to a tree, and that was that. (People said he must have sent the money home to Germany—to relatives, maybe, or maybe as "conscience money." Dad thinks he just needed it to live on.)

A quarry sounds like a funny place to ride, but the actual gravel pit is in the middle of a long, flat stretch of land that runs alongside a kind of bluff above the highway, with the woods curving around in a big semicircle at the back. Mr. Schuller used to graze some sheep there before the quarrying, and the turf has stayed short and springy, as if the sheep had cropped all the growth out of it. Or maybe it was always that way, the soil being so dry and gravelly. I used to take Max there quite a lot after Dad made sure it was okay with Mr. Schuller, and it was a super place to ride. Of course you still had to go in a kind of circle, but it was really more of a long, flat oval—almost like being on a race track, I used to think. At least it will feel like that on Tracker, if I can just find a way to get him there.

The reason I stopped going to the quarry was that a housing development got built along the back side of Mr. Schuller's woods. From our house you used to be able to ride almost in a straight line down over the fields as far as the old Whitman place, where you'd bear left along the edge of the woods until you met the old trucking road coming in from the highway. But the land slopes downhill all the way, and when they put in the road for the housing development, they left such a steep bank on this side that only a goat could get down it. The land there is part ledge, so they had to blast in some places; in others they put up concrete retaining walls. It's such a long way around to the quarry by the main road that I gave up on it, and in fact more or less forgot about it. There were still plenty of places to ride then.

But now . . . I'd never take Tracker around by road, not only because of the distance but also because you have to go along the highway for the last part. What I didn't realize until I studied Larry's map is that when they added some more houses to that development a couple of years ago they also added another road. It cuts in from the left and meets the first road just at the edge of the Whitman property. Well, it's not the Whitman property any more, there's another name now on the mailbox out on Pheasant Ridge Road. When Mom and I drove by there the other day she said how nice it was that at least one of the big old places hadn't been cut up. Actually it's not that much bigger than ours, except that the house is fancier, a square white Colonial with the date 1760 over the front door. There's a lot of lawn and some big shade trees fronting on the road, but the property narrows toward the rear, like a piece of pie. I used to cut across at the very back through a small cow pasture. There was a gate on one side and a ditch on the other, narrow enough for Max to jump (not that he ever liked the idea), but deep enough to keep in the cows.

If the gate is still there we shouldn't have any trouble getting through. But the important thing is that we won't have to go very far on a main road. After only a mile or so on Millbrook Road (that's the one that runs past our house) we can turn off onto Oak Hill Lane, and then it's just a zig and a zag to get to the new development road.

While I'm changing into my jeans and writing a note for Mom—"Gone riding, back around 4"—I worry about whether I should try to phone the new people in the Whitman house, not only to find out about the gate, but also to make sure they won't mind me riding across their land. Not that they'll even see me, probably, I don't think the Whitmans ever did. But anyway, I can't remember their name. I could call Mom at the Lehrmans', I guess, but I don't really want her to know where I'm going, in case it doesn't work out. As for old Mr. Schuller—well, I can't call him because he doesn't have a phone. I can only hope it's still all right for me to ride there after all this time. Anyway, I don't think you can see the quarry land from his shack, which is back up in the woods at the far end. Besides, Dad said that Mr. Schuller's become a bit deaf lately, so he may not even know I'm there.

Tess is still lying under the forsythia bush, panting. I fill up her water bowl and bring it out to her and give her a pat. It's sad to think that out of the three dogs we used to have, only Tess, the oldest, is still around. Our little Corgi got hit by a car out on the road almost opposite our driveway; and Moor, our black Lab, was picked up by the dog warden so many times for wandering that we finally gave him away to a man upstate who wanted a hunting dog. (Moor's idea of retrieving something was to go pick it up and then keep going, but we didn't tell the man that.)

The dog warden never used to bother about Moor until all the new people started moving in. He didn't chase chickens or bother livestock, in fact all he was usually looking for was a new pond to swim in. But then we started getting complaints, mostly from people who just didn't like the idea of finding a strange dog on their property. One complaint was from a woman who found Moor paddling around in her brand-new swimming pool and practically had hysterics. In fact, she called the police. We all thought that was pretty funny, including the dog warden. But when he said we'd have to keep Moor tied up from then on, we decided we'd rather give him away.

"Good girl, Tess," I say, turning away and heading for the paddock. The sky to the northwest is thick with muddy-looking clouds, and I can hear a distant mutter of thunder. But there's no wind to move the clouds. In fact, there's hardly any air stirring. The leaves of the big pear tree hang motionless, and even the mocking bird has shut up for a change. I figure the forecast is right and if we do get a storm it won't be till evening. Both horses are at the near end of the fence, looking at me. "Come on, John," I say as I go past and walk on up the track toward the barn, not daring to look over my shoulder. I can hear John plodding along after me, and pray that Tracker is following him. It's a dirty trick, but it's one that sometimes works.

Sure enough, when I let myself in the gate at the far end, Tracker is at John's heels. I grab Tracker's halter and lead him into his stall, while John looks at me sadly. I feel bad that I didn't bring a carrot or at least a handful of grass for him, but today I didn't want to waste time fooling around trying to catch Tracker. As it is, I find that Tracker's been rolling in the dirt, and I have to spend a while brushing him off before I can saddle him. He stands quietly, as he always does once he's in his stall, but he doesn't look exactly enthusiastic. "Okay," I tell him, "I know it's a hot day, and I know I'm not Shelby, but you're still my horse, and we're still going places together." Tracker turns his head and looks at me gravely. Suddenly there's a lump in my throat. "You're going to get to stretch your legs, boy," I say softly. "You're going to get to *run* for a change."

John moves along the fence beside us as we go down the track. In another minute he'll start his whinnying and pacing, but there won't be anyone around to hear him except old Tess. I relax in the saddle, enjoying the feel of Tracker's smooth, elastic step, and realize it's been almost two weeks since I last rode him—not since that bad time on Bayberry Lane. In some ways Tracker's walk is his best gait. If we lived out West (a favorite dream of mine) we could probably take off for days at a time, camping at night under the stars with only a hoot-owl or maybe a distant coyote to break the silence, not a motorcycle or a truck for miles and miles. . . .

Mom has left her wheelbarrow beside the driveway where she was cleaning out under the peony bushes, with the head of a big iron rake sticking out at an angle. Tracker doesn't even give it a glance as we go by—a good sign, I think. This heavy air makes some creatures twitchy (I listen to the sudden scream of a jay and the nervous twittering of sparrows in the big mock-orange bush), but on Tracker it seems to act like a warm bath, soothing him and slowing down his reactions. When we get to a place where he can run, though, he'll be full of energy, I think hopefully. He won't need any urging then.

He pricks up his ears as we turn left at the end of the driveway, thinking maybe he's going to the front field after all, even if I'm not Shelby—the entrance is diagonally across the road. Usually when I take Tracker on a long ride, we head the other way, toward town, where there are more secondary roads to choose from along the way. But I guide him firmly past the field and on up the hill. After a look over his shoulder Tracker faces front, letting his head droop, plodding along resignedly—exaggerating each step, I think with a grin. His whole body says as plainly as words, "Oh, well, here we go again." But at least it's better than nerves.

We pass the Clayborne farmhouse on our right at the brow of the hill—I notice there's a shiny new swingset where the old chicken-run used to be—and then the row of new houses fronting on the road, with other houses dotted around in the fields behind them. At least when you put up houses in the woods people can have some privacy. Here you can't even put out the garbage without everybody taking notice. Some of the owners have planted trees and hedges, but of course it'll be years before they amount to anything. One house sits inside a rectangle of little evergreens planted close together. If they ever grow up tall, the people will have plenty of privacy, all right, but it will be a pretty weird-looking place to live in.

But at least the people here are sort of permanent, or anyway hope to be. There are carpenters and plumbers, a few schoolteachers, a young policeman and his family . . . people who're involved in the growth of the town. Not like the ones in the newer, more expensive houses—the executive types, Larry calls them, who only expect to live here for three or four years before they're transferred somewhere else, and who don't have any stake in the place. They're the ones who'll ruin it, Larry says, without even knowing or caring. It's just another address to them.

The sun is trying to come through in a white haze overhead, and it's hotter than ever, no breeze even here on the top of the hill. I'm sweating in my old tank-top shirt, and deerflies are nipping my bare arms and neck. I put fly stuff on Tracker, but forgot to put any on myself. He isn't sweating at all, I notice. Whatever I may feel about Shelby and her workouts I have to admit Tracker is in great condition.

The road dips down into a little valley. I can hear a car coming along behind us, and then another appears over the crest of the next hill. I rein Tracker over to the side of the road and we wait for them to pass each other. Maybe the driver on our side will have sense enough to slow down, seeing a horse and rider, but you can't count on that any more. Tracker stands tense, not even taking a swipe at the young leaves of an alder sapling beside him. I can't really blame him. At least there's room here to get out of the way; more than once we've been forced to scramble down into drainage ditches or up slippery banks by drivers who, I guess, expect us to just vanish while they go by. Some of them even honk their horns, which is really intelligent. Almost as bad are the cars that do slow down and then creep along at your heels, as if they're afraid to pass. That really bugs Tracker.

But these two cars just whiz past, paying no attention at all, maybe not even seeing us. Tracker sidles a few steps and flares his nostrils, hating the sound and the smell. It takes some urging to get him to go forward again, and now he's not dopey any more, his ears are alert for the sound of another car or truck or motorcycle, whatever might be coming at him next. My heart sinks, but I remind myself that it's been a couple of weeks since we've been out on the road. Maybe he forgets all about the cars and the bad noises in between times. For Tracker's sake, I hope so.

We climb the next hill.

9

"Okay, Tracker," I say as I see our turnoff up ahead, "we're coming to a firehouse, and there's a big red shiny fire engine inside it. But it's an old one, it's just there for show. It isn't going anywhere, and there aren't any sirens or whistles to worry about, not like at the firehouse downtown. I'll let you take a good look at it, and then we'll go on by, okay?"

I feel silly talking to him like this, but there's a big bottled-gas truck pulling onto the road in front of us from a driveway on our left, and I'm hoping to distract him a little. At least he keeps one ear cocked back for the sound of my voice, and only shudders a little as the truck turns onto the road with a whine of gears and lumbers away ahead of us, leaving a cloud of blue exhaust hanging in the still air. Actually, I *am* a little worried about the fire engine, which is one of those weird-looking antiques with big bulging headlights and a glittering radiator that looks like a mouthful of shark's teeth. Sometimes a stationary object seems more threatening to a horse than one that's moving, maybe because there's no way of telling what it might suddenly *do*.

We turn right, going along one side of a grass triangle that has the old firehouse at its far end. It takes me a moment to realize that the big door is closed, the fire engine safely hidden from sight. I shake my head at myself and let my body slump a little in the saddle. I can feel Tracker relax too, maybe partly because we've left the main road for this leafy lane, maybe partly because in spite of myself I was letting him feel some of my own tension.

That's the worst thing you can do, of course. All the books say so. They also say you shouldn't baby a nervous horse. You should take him briskly and firmly past (or over, or under) any obstacle that bothers him. Above all, you should never humor him by getting off and leading him. Which is all very well, but sometimes, when I've managed to force Tracker past something that scares him by pretending to ignore his feelings, he'll be in such a state of nerves afterward that the least little thing will spook him—a brightly painted mailbox, a sprinkler going on someone's lawn, a screen door banging.

It seems better to let him have his fear and get it over with. Or get on the other side of it, anyway. At least that way he knows I understand.

"Good boy, Tracker," I say, for no particular reason except that I'm feeling happier now. It's a little cooler here under the trees, and the only sounds are the good familiar jingle of the bridle and the creak of leather and the steady clop-clop of Tracker's hooves on the weathered blacktop of the lane. Even the thunder seems to have died down. From here on I can't think of anything that could cause trouble—anything I have to plan for, anyhow. I can stop acting like a soldier in enemy territory—maybe that sounds silly, but it's the way I feel sometimes—and just be what I want to be: a girl riding her horse along a quiet country road.

And for a while that's the way it is. The lane curves downhill past a couple of houses set back in the woods, and then it runs straight for a quarter of a mile or so until it dead-ends on Longmeadow Road. Along this stretch there's a kind of natural track beside the blacktop, just earth and leafmold, and I put Tracker into his lovely, easy canter—not the tight short gait he's been taught for jumping, but his old, free rocking-horse stride. He blows gently through his nostrils when I have to rein him up at last, letting me know his pleasure. "Just wait till we get to the quarry," I tell him, patting his neck. "Then you can really take off."

Now we have just a short zag to the left on Longmeadow, which, according to the map, meets the new development road coming in at an angle. There are more houses here, but no traffic except for a couple of small boys dawdling along on their bikes. Tracker looks at them with interest. He likes kids, and bikes don't bother him, maybe because he can see the humans working them—not like cars and trucks, or even motorcycles, where the rider hardly looks human anyway.

One of the boys stops to watch us as we walk sedately by. "Is that your horse?" he asks. At the moment it seems like a dumb question. "Sure," I say. "He's nice," the kid says shyly, and I turn in my saddle to smile at him, still balancing his bike at the side of the road to watch us go by.

I can feel how the brief canter has relaxed Tracker. Even when we come to a gatepost with a big bunch of balloons tied to it—some little kid must be having a birthday party—he only eyes them curiously, and goes by without changing his stride. I glance at my watch as we approach the crossroad, where a new metal signpost announces Beaver Ledge Lane. (That's the kind of name the developers are always thinking up. Never mind that beavers don't live on ledges and that the nearest stream is half a mile away.) We've been gone about twenty minutes, and I figure another ten, at most, should get us to the quarry. That's not bad; and except for the first part along Millbrook Road it's really quite a nice ride.

Because of the angle we have to take a sharp right turn onto Beaver Ledge Lane. Some tall cedar trees block our view of the corner house. On the other side of the trees we come practically face to face with the biggest German shepherd I've ever seen. It's standing stock still at the end of the driveway, growling deep in its throat. Before I can react, it lunges at us, snarling and baring its teeth—and is brought up short at the end of a heavy chain. Am I glad to see that chain.

But Tracker only sees the lunging dog. He rears and twists sideways, coming down with his forefeet in the middle of the road—or rather, the middle of our side of the road. It's a good thing these new roads have to be made wider than most of the old ones, because at that moment a yellow sports car comes whipping through the intersection without stopping or even slowing. It veers around us, but then has to cut back in, with a squeal of tires, to avoid a car that's backing out of a driveway across the road. In a moment it is gone. I have my hands full with Tracker, who is wheeling and plunging and fighting the bit, but I am dimly aware of the dog still snarling behind us and of a woman getting out of the car across the way and coming toward us.

"Can I help?" she calls.

"No, it's all right," I say breathlessly, finally getting Tracker under some kind of control. "He's just a little scared, that's all."

"I should think he might be!" The woman stares in the direction of the yellow car. "Imagine driving like that on a road where there are kids and dogs and—well, we don't get many horses here, but— Thor, you stop that!" This to the German shepherd, who is sitting on his haunches now, still growling and showing his teeth. She shakes her head. "If that was my dog I'd have him put away. Guard dog! He's just plain vicious, if you ask me."

Tracker is standing still now, trembling and sweating. I stroke his withers gently, and ease him forward a few steps onto the grass verge of the road, putting a few more yards between us and the dog. "They can be nice dogs, though, shepherds," I say, partly just for something to say to this woman, who was nice enough, after all, to get out of her car and see if she could help, and partly in the hope that my conversational tone will soothe Tracker a little.

"Sure, if you train 'em right," she agrees. "But people like that"—she nods scornfully at the house, not

96

bothering to lower her voice, and I see now that the garage is empty, no one's home—"they never had a dog before, until they moved here. They figure they're way out in the country—some country! I grew up on a farm, honey, and I know what country is. So they need a big fierce dog to protect their kids. Well, he does that all right, won't let anyone else near 'em, including their own playmates. They had to put him on the chain after he bit one little girl. Lucky he didn't go for her throat."

I feel a little sick. It's not only her words, but also the heat and exertion and what I now realize was a narrow escape, not only for Tracker and me, but also for the woman. If the sportscar had hit her car it would have been our fault in a way. . . . I swallow hard and wipe the damp hair back from my forehead.

The woman notices. Her eyes are shrewd and sharp behind her blue-rimmed glasses. "You sure you're okay, honey? That horse of yours looks pretty shook up, all lathered like he is. Gave me a scare too, slamming on the brakes the way I had to, but at least my car don't know the difference. Maybe you'd better head back the way you came. This isn't much of a place for horseback riding. We get a lot of through traffic, even though the road's posted against it—people cutting over to the state highway by way of Sprucewood Drive, like that maniac just now."

I explain that I'm turning off soon, heading toward

the woods. The woman looks doubtful, but shrugs and says, "Well, I guess you know your own business. I'd ask you to stop in for a cold drink, except I got my week's marketing to do, and the bank before it closes." She gives a sudden chuckle. "Don't know where you'd tether your horse, though. Maybe to the carriage lamp, if it ain't hollow inside, the way they make things these days. Anyhow, you come this way again, you stop and say hello, okay?"

I assure her that I will, and she goes back and gets into her car and drives off with a parting wave. Feeling better, warmed by her concern, I touch my heels to Tracker's sides and we move forward again. But it's a shaky kind of progress we make along the length of Beaver Ledge Lane. Tracker's step is jerky, and I can see the whites of his eyes when he tosses his head from side to side. When another car comes along he's ready to bolt. Luckily this one is going at a normal speed and doesn't do anything out of the ordinary. I keep a tight grip on the reins, leaning forward at the same time to pat his neck and talk to him.

"Poor old Tracker," I say—and suddenly I mean it, suddenly I'm full of pity for him and disgust at myself. What am I trying to do to him anyway, my strong, proud, sturdy horse? You would hardly recognize him now in this sweating, trembling creature who's ready to shy at his own shadow.

I tell myself it will be different when we get to

the quarry. The quarry will make it all worthwhile—not just for me, but for Tracker too.

Because of the heat, and maybe the threat of a storm—thunder is rumbling again in the northwest—most people seem to be staying indoors. All the houses here are set back at the same distance from the road, with identical squares of front lawn, as though they'd all been seeded and rolled and watered and mowed at the same time. The only differences are in the bushes people have chosen—azaleas or rhododendrons, laurels or junipers—and in the way they've laid out their front walks. Some are gravel, some are asphalt, some are plain cement. I notice one made of flagstones, another that's made of cobblestones and looks hard to walk on, and another of bricks laid out in a herringbone pattern.

I make myself look at all these things as we go by so as to keep from worrying about the next stage of our route—the Whitmans' back pasture and the gate that may or may not be there, locked or unlocked. Also I have a nutty idea that by thinking dull, ordinary thoughts I may be able to help get Tracker back to normal too. A few houses before Beaver Ledge Lane runs into Sprucewood Drive, the original development road, there's a man out playing badminton in his front yard with two little girls. I rein Tracker in so that he can watch, in line with my idea of focusing on something ordinary and everyday. At first he shifts his feet nervously, but then he gets interested. He stands quietly, ears pricked high, watching the peculiar humans running around on the grass and batting a small white object back and forth over a net. When he isn't scared Tracker is just as curious as the next horse.

They didn't hear us coming because we've been keeping to the grass at the side of the road, and besides, they've been making a lot of noise themselves, laughing and yelling. But now one of the little girls runs over toward the driveway to retrieve the badminton bird, and she looks up and sees us. Her eyes widen and she says, "Oh, Daddy, look!"

Immediately the other little girl comes running. "Oh, isn't he pretty! Can we have a ride? Will you give us a ride on him?"

Tracker backs off a little and steps sideways, but I'm glad to feel that it's just ordinary wariness, not real nerves. I smile and shake my head at the little girls, but my smile fades when the man calls out sharply, "Careful, Linda, don't get too close, he might kick you." In the first place, Tracker hardly ever kicks, and in the second, he'd never knowingly hurt anyone, least of all a child.

I give the man what I hope is a cold stare and we move on, past the remaining two houses, to the corner. I was right to have stopped, though. Tracker is reacting to things more normally now, taking in his surroundings instead of being overwhelmed by them. When I urge him up the slight embankment onto the strip of wasteland that separates Sprucewood Drive from the Whitman property he flicks an ear back as if to say, "Are you sure this is where you want to go?" but makes no protest. And now he has to concentrate on picking his way. There are prickly cedar seedlings here, and tangles of purple vetch among the clumps of tall grass. I leave him to it, getting my own bearings from a glimpse of the roof of the house off at an angle to my left, half buried among its shade trees. I fix my own gaze ahead to where the fence should be—and, I hope, the gate.

There isn't any gate, but neither is there a fence any more. They've taken it down, posts and all. The little back pasture has been recently mown, cut close, as though they might be planning to make a lawn out of it. Or maybe they're going to put something here. There's already a pool, I remember. A rose garden? A tennis court? I grin to myself, thinking that would really give Tracker something to look at, provided they didn't mind our riding past it. That reminds me that I'm trespassing. I resist the impulse to hunch my shoulders and instead sit loose and easy in the saddle as we start across the pasture, as if I have every right to be here. I can hear a radio playing somewhere in the direction of the house, but I don't think anyone has seen us.

Halfway across, I notice that they've also taken down the barbed-wire fencing at the end of the pasture that used to keep the cows from wandering off into the woods there. I hesitate a moment, thinking maybe we could turn off into the woods now and get to the trucking road that much sooner. But probably it's better to go the way I remember—across the ditch and through another patch of scrub to meet the woods where they curve around and thin almost to a point. Next time we can try the other way.

The ditch has gotten so overgrown with weeds and wildflowers you'd hardly know it was there. I'm glad I do know—it's no place for a horse to discover by accident. It's kind of pretty, though. I pick a spot where a mass of wild roses foams over the edge and put Tracker at it. It's just a baby jump for him, of course. He sails over it with several feet to spare.

And then, suddenly, he's squealing and plunging, trying to rear, but held down by something I can't see.

I fling myself off his back. "Stand, Tracker, stand!" I yell, as he screams again in pain. There is a great snarl of barbed wire lying in the grass, and I have jumped Tracker right into the middle of it.

10

I am shaking and crying so much I can hardly see. The wire tears at my jeans as I crouch to examine Tracker's legs, but I don't even feel it. I can hear myself still telling Tracker to stand—but already some survival instinct has taken over: he is quiet now, as if he understands that fighting the wire will only make things worse. He shudders violently, trembling in every muscle, but at least he makes no effort to move his forelegs. They are bleeding in a dozen places below the knees, where the ugly barbs have torn into his flesh, and the wire still surrounds him like a bristling hedge.

"Okay, boy, take it easy." I hardly know what I'm saying, but I know he needs to hear the sound of my voice. It's not as bad as it looks, just scratches really, nothing too deep. "We'll have you out of this in just a minute. Just don't try to move. . . ."

I reach for one of the strands of wire and then let my hand drop helplessly. I can't expect Tracker to go on standing motionless while I untangle it strand by strand, and any sudden movement will only enmesh him further. "Damn them!" I say wildly as I straighten up. "Damn anyone who'd leave barbed wire lying around! Stupid damn people, don't they know anything? They're criminals, that's all they are, and if they've hurt you they'll be sorry, they'll pay for it!"

I'm so choked with rage and anguish I can't go on, which is just as well, because this kind of talk won't help Tracker, and neither will my tears. But I don't know what to do. I stroke Tracker's bowed neck as he stands with his head hanging, and try to get hold of myself. At least his rear legs are clear; only his forelegs came down into the wire. If I could get him to lift one foot at a time, maybe I could clear a bit more space for him. But no, the wire's too tough. It's snagged fast in the grass, and there's too much of it. I'd probably only make things worse. . . .

"What's the matter with your horse? Oh! Oh, my gosh!"

I didn't hear her coming because she's barefoot— a girl about my age or maybe a little older, wearing a bright yellow bikini; she's very tanned, and has long, dark, pulled-back hair, and wide brown eyes that stare at Tracker and then down at the vicious tangle of wire.

"Watch it!" I say sharply, and she steps back hastily, thinking I mean the wire. I couldn't care less about her bare feet, I just don't want her to startle Tracker. "Please just stay quiet," I beg. "If he moves—"

"Oh. Yes, I see what you mean. Is he hurt bad, do you think?"

"Not yet," I say grimly. "But I've got to get this stuff away from him. Do you have some wire cutters? Or pliers, even? No, this is heavy-duty wire, I'll need cutters." At least my mind is beginning to work again.

But the girl looks blank. She turns her head toward the house—I notice now that there's a plank laid across the ditch farther along, which must be how she got across—and says vaguely, "Well, there're some shears and things in the garden shed. . . ."

"Not shears," I say impatiently. "Wire cutters—you know, they're heavy iron things with big sharp blades."

"I don't know. My dad sold off most of the farm-type tools when we moved in, but there might be something like that around somewhere . . . only no one else is home, and I wouldn't even know where to start looking." Seeing the expression on my face she offers hesitantly, "I could go call a vet for you. Wouldn't that be the best thing to do? I mean, he'd bring wire cutters with him, wouldn't he?"

At least she's heard of vets, I think dully, that's something. Unfortunately the only horse vet left in the area, Dr. Innis, is a good half-hour's drive away from here, maybe more if he's out on a call somewhere and has to be reached. And the important thing right now is to get Tracker out of the wire as soon as possible. My mind races, thinking back to the houses we passed on Beaver Ledge Lane. It's unlikely that anyone there would have such a thing as a pair of wire cutters just lying around the place. But suddenly I think of someone who would.

I look at the girl again, and make up my mind. She may not know anything about horses, but there's a look of real concern in her dark eyes; she has a soft voice and a quiet manner, and at least she hasn't fainted at the sight of a little blood. Besides, I don't have much choice.

"Look," I say, handing her the reins, "you stay with Tracker, will you? I think I know where I can get some cutters. It'll take me"—I calculate rapidly—"ten minutes, maybe fifteen. Just keep talking to him, anything that comes into your head. If he gets restless, tell him, 'Stand, Tracker,' in a very firm voice."

I close my eyes for a moment, not wanting to think about what could happen if Tracker comes out of the kind of daze he seems to be in right now. His head is still hanging in that defeated way that twists at my heart, and he isn't so much trembling now as quivering. He's in some kind of shock, I realize; but at least the cuts seem to have stopped bleeding, and if he doesn't mess with the wire any more, the damage won't be too bad. A page of my horse-care manual prints itself before my eyes: to prevent infection wash with saline solution, then apply antiseptic cream or ointment—

Later, I'll worry about all that later. I kick off my boots. "Here, you'd better put these on. Even if they don't fit they'll be better than nothing, and I can run faster without them."

The girl blinks at me. "Couldn't you just call the person?" she asks. "I mean—"

"He doesn't have a phone. Be a good boy, Tracker," I say, giving him a quick light pat and trying to sound casual and confident. "I'll be back as soon as I can."

I'm just turning away when there's a growl of thunder off in the distance, and I see the girl stiffen. "It's okay," I tell her. "The storm's still a long way off, and Tracker isn't scared of thunder."

"No," she says, trying to smile. "But I am. It's all right," she adds quickly, seeing me hesitate. "You go ahead. I'll stay with him and keep him quiet. I guess it's our fault about the wire, isn't it."

It's not a question. I take a deep breath—but what's the point? I shrug. "Well, we were trespassing," I say. And then I'm off.

At first I don't run too fast, partly because I don't want Tracker to watch me and get alarmed, partly because the ground is uneven here, lumpy with tussocks of grass and weeds and laced with briars that rip at my feet through the thin socks I'm wearing. It won't do any of us much good if I sprain an ankle. But when I get to the trucking road I stop to peel off my socks and prepare to sprint. It's a lot more overgrown than I remember, just a track now. It runs slightly uphill, but at least it's level underfoot and straight, and I'm able to get up some speed. In fact, I think crazily as I pound along, I'm probably going faster now than I ever did on old Max when I used to trot him along this last stretch.

Suddenly I feel space opening up around me, and there it is—the wide plateau with the long curving line of woods on my right, the rocky ledge of the bluff on my left, and in the middle, the crater of the gravel pit inside its ragged collar of heaped dirt and sand. Today there is no glare of sunlight on rock and mica, no hard blue sky overhead. (I used to pretend this was a place out West, a mesa maybe, or a butte, whatever a butte is exactly.) Instead the sky is gray and sullen, and the stunted grass surrounding the quarry glows an unnatural green in the dull light.

I leave the track and pick my way over a scree of rocks and boulders left by the bulldozer that made the road, and then pause to get my bearings. You can't see Mr. Schuller's house from here, let alone the path that leads to it through the woods, but I'm pretty sure it's just about opposite where I am now. Which is quicker, the flat route along the bluff, or the wider, more shelving stretch of land to my right? It's probably shorter along the bluff, but the turf on the right looks thicker and smoother—less chance of my stubbing a toe on a rock and falling flat.

Once I'm running again, I discover that what seems springy and smooth under a horse's hooves feels pretty rough and scratchy to bare human feet. There are sharp little stones and tiny thistles, and once I just manage to avoid stepping on a miniature nettle. And needless to say, the distance seems about ten times as long. Two hundred yards, three hundred? I ought to know because of all the distance running Miss Lowrie made us do in gym class this year to get us ready for our fitness tests. I wish she could see me now. Whatever the record is I must be breaking it.

I think of Miss Lowrie as I run, and of Barry Slater, a skinny little kid who surprised everyone by making the longest broad jump of anyone in school—anything to keep from thinking about Tracker. The air seems almost too heavy to breathe, almost solid, lodged like a thick gray mass in my chest, weighing me down from inside as my body pushes against it on the outside. By the time I get to the far side of the quarry I'm gasping at every step, and there's a funny kind of pain behind my eyeballs, so that the dark wall of woods ahead of me blurs and quivers and I can't see the path anywhere.

I make myself stop. When my vision clears—part of the trouble turns out to be that sweat is literally pouring into my eyes—I still can't see the path. Mr. Schuller is pretty old now, I think despairingly. Probably he never uses it any more, never comes this way— why should he? I search the trees again for some sign of an opening, but this is second-growth woods, with thick underbrush, and I can't see a gap in it anywhere. If I have to waste time blundering around in the woods . . .

I think of yelling, but then I remember what my father said about Mr. Schuller's deafness. I try to visualize where the cabin must be, but I've never actually seen it—only the path leading in on this side, and the long, narrow driveway twisting up and out of sight from the highway below.

I'm about to plunge into the undergrowth at random when something on the ground catches my eye. It's a bit of stained white plastic, no more than an inch long. It takes me a moment to realize that it's the tip of one of those little cigars Mr. Schuller is always smoking. Or used to smoke. It occurs to me that it's been a long time since I've seen him, at least to speak to, and that he may not even know who I am any more. On horseback, maybe, but on foot, red-faced and dirty, with tangled hair, rushing in like this on his cherished privacy? . . .

Never mind. If he has wire cutters he'll lend them to me. And he must have them, from the days when he used to keep sheep. I try not to think how many years ago that was. Instead I carefully study the ground in front of me and make out the thin line of a path leading into the woods, no more than a faint parting in the curled young ferns and the ground pine under the trees.

I push my way along it as fast as I can, ignoring poison ivy and brambles, jumping over fallen limbs and branches, scrambling over the thick trunk of a big dead tree. And there on the other side of the trunk—as if the trunk had been put there as a barrier—is a small clearing, and in the clearing is a cabin. It's so smothered in vines and creepers it looks more like something that grew by itself than a place that someone built. In fact, it's kind of spooky in here, so quiet and still, not even a bird calling. I almost welcome a sudden rumble of thunder—it proves the rest of the world is still out there after all—until I remember the girl back there with Tracker. I just hope she doesn't start to panic; or if she does, that she'll manage to hide it from him. . . .

Meanwhile I'm adding my own noise to the scene, knocking on what seems to be the front door—politely at first, then loudly when there's no answer. I know Mr. Schuller is here, I can see his pickup truck parked in a kind of makeshift carport on the far side of the clearing. I bang my fists on the door and yell, "Mr. Schuller!" Still there's no answer, except from a squirrel chattering at me from the branch of a pine tree. I look at my watch: seven minutes since I left Tracker. It doesn't seem possible, it feels more like seven hours, but it's still too much.

I circle the cabin. Tacked onto a lean-to kitchen area is another, smaller shed, which must be where he keeps his tools and other gear. I try the door. There's a bolt, but no lock, and it swings open easily enough. Once my eyes get used to the darkness I see that I'm right, it is a toolshed—one of the neatest I've ever seen, though not the cleanest. There are cobwebs everywhere, and dust, and choking, musty-smelling heat as if the door hasn't been opened in months; but everything seems exactly in its place, from the pickax and crowbar and other heavy gear standing in one corner to the smaller tools hanging on nails along the inner wall.

It takes me only a few seconds to spot the wire

cutters, a big, sturdy pair with red-painted handles. I balance it gratefully in my hand, fighting the impulse to just rush off with it like a thief. Unwillingly, I notice the stub of a pencil and some sandpaper on the workbench. I could, I should, write on the back of it— just a quick note, to explain . . .

There is a rasping cough behind me. I wheel around to find Mr. Schuller swaying in the doorway, blinking at me from behind his wire-rimmed glasses. He is wearing his usual uniform of khaki shirt and pants, but they are stained and rumpled and seem to sag on his thin frame as if he's lost a lot of weight recently.

"Oh, Mr. Schuller!" I advance toward him, into the light where he can see me, and then I back up a step. Even from a few feet away I can smell the reek of liquor on his breath. Oh my gosh, what have I gotten into now? If only I'd been half a minute quicker— I hold out the wire cutters and say as calmly as I can (but loudly too, remembering his deafness), "I needed to borrow these, and I couldn't make you hear when I knocked on the door. My horse is caught in some barbed wire. I'm—"

"I know," he interrupts, nodding. "Young Kate." He hasn't missed my moment of recoil. "Cognac," he explains, and presses a hand to his side. "For the pain. No matter. Your horse—where?"

"At the Whitmans', on the other side of the quarry. If I can just borrow your cutters, I'll be as quick as

I can. . . ." I hesitate, in spite of my desperate need to be off. Mr. Schuller really does look terrible, his skin all yellow-gray and dry. "If you're sick, maybe I could call a doctor for you from there."

"We take the truck," he announces, ignoring this last. "It's quicker." I give him a startled glance, but he is looking down at my bare feet, and I follow his gaze. I didn't realize they were bleeding. Me and Tracker both, I think forlornly. Before I can say anything—is Mr. Schuller in any shape to drive?—he manages a smile that isn't quite a grimace. "I am not so very drunk, child. Come."

Without waiting to see if I am following he turns away and takes down a bunch of keys from a nail outside the kitchen door. Slowly and unsteadily he walks across the clearing to the pickup truck.

11

I guess I'm having some kind of delayed reaction. I hardly feel the bumps and jolts as we careen down the steep driveway. Even when we turn onto the highway and I'm aware in some part of my mind that the truck is weaving back and forth more than it should, it doesn't seem to matter. All that matters is that Mr. Schuller is willing to do this for me, and that I'm on my way back to Tracker.

I sit on the edge of the worn seat, clutching the cold, heavy wire cutters in my sweaty hands. Luckily, it's a short distance and there isn't much traffic. Soon after we pass the old quarry entrance we turn off the highway onto Pheasant Ridge Road. The Whitman house is the second on the left. I start to point, but Mr. Schuller is already hauling the wheel around, nosing the truck onto the gravel driveway under the big trees. I notice how thin his fingers are, skeleton fingers almost, gripping the wheel.

There is still no one home except the girl, judging from the emptiness of the three-car garage. Mr. Schuller stops the truck in front of it and sits back with a grunt. Again he presses a hand to his side. There are beads of sweat on his gaunt cheekbones, but he says calmly, "You have a good horse now, young Kate. I know, your father tells me. Gloves there." He nods at the glove compartment and gestures impatiently when I just stare at it. I open it—gloves in the glove compartment, sure enough, I think, a little hysterically. But they are heavy work gloves, something I haven't even thought of. I hesitate, my hand on the door. Mr. Schuller looks even worse than he did before, as if he might pass out.

But now his voice is impatient too. "Go. Run to the horse. I rest here a little while. Then I come too."

"But Mr. Schuller— Oh, thank you for driving me here, thank you for everything, but you shouldn't. I mean, there's a girl with him, with my horse, and between us we can manage okay. You're sick, you can't—"

116

"I can do what I will," he interrupts, and turns his head to look at me. There's something like a glint of amusement in his pale eyes behind the glasses. "Have your care for the horse, not old Schuller. He survives. Now go. Run."

So I do, clutching the gloves and the cutters, across a smooth, green lawn where a flower border makes a bright blur of color against my right cheek, past the blue glitter of the swimming pool—the radio is still playing, a tinny, meaningless sound in the heavy air—onto the narrow stretch of lawn that ends at the pasture. Gloves in the glove compartment, where else? I think again, idiotically, as I run; and my first thought at the sight of the girl and Tracker, standing in the field just as I left them, is how ridiculous she looks wearing her yellow bikini and my old cowboy boots.

I remember to look for the plank across the ditch, and also to slow down so as not to startle Tracker, and that sobers me. The girl has her back to me and hasn't seen me yet; but now Tracker does. He turns his head and gives a low whinny. I notice that she has a shorter grip on the reins now, as if maybe Tracker had started trying to move again.

"I got a ride back," I explain breathlessly as she turns around in surprise. "Is everything okay? He hasn't cut himself any more?"

"No. He got sort of restless after a while, but I told

him to stand, the way you said, and he did. It's as if he knew he had to wait for you." She smiles, but I see how strained her face looks, as if it's gone pale beneath her tan. Except for that moment in the clearing, I've hardly noticed the thunder, but I guess it's been grumbling away all along—a bit louder now, maybe, though the storm is still miles away.

Well, the sooner I get to work the sooner she can go back to her pool and her radio. I just hope she has enough sense to get away from the water if there's any lightning. I pull on the heavy gloves and say, "Just hold him steady a few minutes more, okay? This shouldn't take long."

It doesn't. The heavy blades bite easily through the tough wire, and in no time at all I've cut the whole tangled mass into small sections that I can pull away and toss into the grass behind me. I'm grateful for Mr. Schuller's gloves. Without them my hands would be in worse shape than my feet. I can feel the cuts and scratches now, stinging and throbbing the way poor Tracker's must be. All the time I'm working I avoid looking at his legs; but now, as I drag the last length of wire away and add it to the pile, I force myself to study them. No fresh bleeding, no swelling that I can see. . . .

I shake my head at myself. It's been—what?— twenty minutes since I jumped Tracker over the ditch, much too soon to tell if there's going to be any serious infection. I wouldn't think so, but still— "Could you get me some salt water?" I ask the girl as I get to my feet and take Tracker's reins from her. "You know, just dump some spoonfuls of salt in a pail of water, or in a big bowl or something, and bring a clean sponge or a rag too. I want to wash off his legs where the cuts are."

She nods uncertainly and then flinches—her whole body tenses, even her bare midriff—as a wave of thunder rolls across the northwest sky. Suddenly I realize the courage it must have taken for her to stand out here all this time, keeping still and calm for Tracker's sake, and I'm ashamed of the way I've been putting her down in my mind. But before I can say anything I see her eyes widen, looking past me. I turn to see Mr. Schuller advancing slowly into the pasture, looking frailer than ever against the background of green lawn and graceful, arching trees. He crosses the plank over the ditch with careful steps and then stops, frowning down at the pile of barbed wire, finally turning his gaze on Tracker.

I realize that Tracker still hasn't moved, as if he can't quite take in the fact that he's free. "Come on, boy," I say, giving him a pat, and lead him over to the old man. His first steps are reluctant, but then, when he realizes his legs still work, his head comes

119

up, his neck curves once more, his ears prick forward. I can practically feel the energy flowing back into his body.

Mr. Schuller watches him and nods. "He moves well. Very nice. A good horse."

I turn belatedly back to the girl. "This is my friend Mr. Schuller," I say. "He lives over there on the other side of the quarry. And this is—" I stop because I still don't know the girl's name.

"Sarah Buckley," she says quickly. I can see she's trying not to stare at Mr. Schuller. He looks better than he did a few minutes ago, but not much. "I'll get the salt water now, okay? And is there anything else—someone I could call, or—"

"Salt water, good," Mr. Schuller interrupts in his brusque way. "But a little salt only, not to hurt too much." With a grunt he bends down to inspect Tracker's legs. He even runs a hand down his pasterns— feeling for warmth, I realize. Tracker blows uneasily through his nostrils, but stands for him.

The girl is still waiting for my answer. "Well, I don't know . . ." I haven't thought this far, only as far as getting Tracker out of the wire. There's no need for a vet, not now anyway, but maybe I should call Pam to see if she could come and van Tracker home. To Mr. Schuller I say, "What do you think about riding him?" When he looks up, puzzled, I explain, remembering to raise my voice, "I could get a van to take him home. You know—a truck, a horse truck."

"No, no." He straightens up with an obvious effort, but his voice is decisive. "Better you ride him. Better for your horse, to keep him from"—he searches for the word—"stiff, the stiffness. For his spirit too. Nerves, I think you say." His eyes behind the glasses catch something in my face. "Better for you too, young Kate, I think," he adds gently.

I nod, knowing he's right. But I can't help dreading the thought of the ride home.

In the silence, the girl—Sarah—looks from one of us to the other. Then she says, "Well, I'll just get the water then. Here, you'd better take these back." She pulls off my boots and holds them out to me with a grin. "I thought *I* had big feet, but yours are even bigger. Good thing I didn't have to run anywhere in these."

I grin back at her. My jaw muscles feel all tight and funny, and I realize it's the first time I've smiled in quite a while. "Hey," I say as she's turning away, "I never introduced myself—Kate Wendall. And I never thanked you. I really do thank you, a whole lot. If you hadn't been here—" I shrug, looking at Tracker.

She shrugs too. "If the wire hadn't been left where it was. . . . Well anyway, it won't be there next time, if you still want to come this way."

Next time.

After a shaky start, when Tracker and I have to get used to being on the move again, the ride home turns out to be no big deal after all, just sort of automatic. Of course it helps that we don't meet another maniac in a sports car, and that the German shepherd's family seems to have come home and put him in the house. But mainly, I guess, I'm just too exhausted to worry the way I usually do. One of the worst things that could happen *has* happened, and we're out of it, and I just don't have any imagination left over for anything else.

Maybe Tracker feels the same way. He plods along, satisfied to be going home but not making a big thing out of it—more like some old farmhorse heading for the barn, I think dully, than my tense, watchful Tracker. He isn't limping at all that I can feel. I'm careful to keep him on the paved surface as we wind our way up Oak Hill Lane so that his cuts and scratches will stay clean and not get bits of dirt or gravel in them; but otherwise I'm more conscious of my own cut-up feet, which probably *are* getting dirty inside my old boots, and which hurt besides. Mr. Schuller insisted on my washing them in the saline solution we used for Tracker, and I'm afraid I wasn't as brave about it as Tracker was, though I did manage to keep from actually howling out loud.

By the time we pass the old firehouse and turn onto Millbrook Road, it's all I can do to stay in the saddle. My shirt is sticking to me with sweat, and a mosquito I picked up on Oak Hill Lane is still with me, whining around my ears and getting into my tangled, damp hair. Not only do my feet hurt, my bare arms are stinging from briar scratches, and one knee throbs where the barbed wire tore through my jeans. In addition to all this, I figure I'll have a royal case of poison ivy in the next day or two. The air is so close and heavy now it feels like a suit of plastic armor.

At the crest of the long hill leading down to our driveway I rein Tracker in for a moment to watch the purple storm clouds beginning to move in over the landscape now, with flickers of lightning in them. The rain will feel good, I think, and the wind. I wish it would come now. I wish the rain would come to drench us both where we stand.

But of course this will be no ordinary summer rain, the kind horses seem to welcome as they stand in their fields and paddocks, enjoying a giant shower bath. Even horses have enough sense to make for their barns and stables when there's lightning in the rain.

I touch my heels to Tracker's sides and we start down the hill. I can see our rooftop now, and the barn, and the field sloping down to the green-rimmed pond, which gleams dully like an old piece of scrap metal, like a flattened-out nickel someone put on a railroad track. Behind us a car starts to pass, and then slows. Tracker's ears twitch, he looks around at the man in the car, who is leaning over from the wheel to say, "Hope you don't have far to go, miss, looks like there's a storm coming."

I thank him and explain we're almost home. He nods and drives on. All at once my eyes are full of tears, I don't know why. Maybe just because the man was nice. But of course I do know why.

"Stop feeling so damn sorry for yourself, Kate Wendall," I say aloud. "Think of Mr. Schuller, for instance." Tracker's head comes up at my angry tone, and I stroke his neck in apology. "Good boy, Tracker," I murmur automatically. "We're almost there, not much farther now."

Mr. Schuller waited until I was mounted on Tracker and then made me a funny, formal little bow. "A safe journey," he said.

I'd been half afraid that Tracker might refuse the ditch, but he didn't; he seemed to jump it without even thinking about it, only looking around at me inquiringly when I reined in on the other side. Mr. Schuller and Sarah stood watching us, Sarah holding the yellow plastic pail of water—the color matched her bikini—and Mr. Schuller grasping the work gloves and the wire cutters that looked too heavy for his brittle hands.

I hesitated, and then I said, "Mr. Schuller, are you

sure you're all right? To drive home, I mean, and—and everything?"

He smiled a little. "It is doctors you are thinking of, is it not, young Kate? Doctors and hospitals and needles to pretend against the pain. No. I make my own journey, in my own way. I have my own space, you see—my little box, you might call it, in which I am accustomed to live." And then he said a strange thing, lifting his head to look at me where I sat on Tracker. I couldn't see his eyes because of the way the light struck flat on the lenses of his glasses; but I could feel something urgent in his gaze, as if he was trying to send me a message. "There is always a way out of the box, you know. But first one must believe that the world is bigger than the box. I was taught otherwise, but you"—he lifted his thin shoulders slightly—"you are young. You will find the way."

Now, as Tracker turns at last into our driveway I think that I will tell my father about Mr. Schuller. Maybe Dad can go see him and persuade him to change his mind about getting help. Or if not, maybe Mr. Schuller will at least be glad of a little company, whatever he may say.

John is at the end of the paddock fence, whinnying a welcome. His brown mane is whipped sideways by a gust of wind that also tosses the heads of the tall delphiniums in my mother's garden, blue as the sky

125

on some other day. Mom's car is in the garage. She's probably been worrying about me, I think dully. But when I look at my watch I find it's only a little after three. I haven't even used up the time I had.

"He *what?*" Pam explodes over the phone. "For God's sake, Kate—! Where on earth were you? How bad is it? Have you called Dr. Innis?"

I explain as briefly as I can, adding that I washed Tracker's legs again when I got home, and put on some antibiotic stuff, and that I don't feel any warmth or swelling.

"Well, it doesn't sound too serious," Pam admits grudgingly. "But I'd like to come over and take a look in the morning, if you don't mind. I mean, whatever you decide about him, that's a good horse, Kate, and really, of all the careless things, riding him into barbed wire—"

I'm tempted to hang up on her. Instead I say wearily, "You don't have to worry, Pam. I won't be doing it again. I'm going to call Shelby now and tell her she can have Tracker." Behind me, at the sink, I can feel Mom go still, letting the water run down unheeded over the lettuce she's washing for a salad. "Also, do you think you might be able to use John at the academy? I really won't have much use for him myself, and anyway, my father's been thinking about getting a milk cow, and maybe some pigs again"—this isn't a fib, it's something Dad has mentioned once or twice, saying he'd pay me to take care of them—"and if he does, he'll probably want to fix the barn over differently. You know, get rid of the box stalls, and maybe the paddock too. . . . Well, I guess that's really up to Shelby, where to board the horses and all, but I just thought I'd let you know."

The storm holds off after all until dinnertime. When it comes it knocks the power out for a couple of hours, and I have to take a candle upstairs with me to light my way to bed. I lie there listening to the rain drumming steadily on the eaves and gurgling in a gutter that probably needs cleaning out, while the thunder rumbles off into another part of the county with a sound like carriage wheels going away.

The earth has what it waited for so breathlessly all day, the coolness and the rain; and already the waiting seems like part of another day.

12

The day before the horses are to leave John gets out of the paddock. I forgot all about the cracked fence-post, but John didn't. A whole section of fencing is down, or partly down, shoved askew toward the next post in line. Shelby is riding Tracker in the front field. Of John there is no sign.

Usually I would go drag some old boards over from the shed beyond the garage and nail together a rough barricade, just something to hold the horses in until Dad gets home and can repair the fence. Today I don't feel like going to the trouble. The horses can stay in their stalls for once. It won't kill them.

First I have to find John, though. The dog leash I lent Shelby is still hanging from the hook by the kitchen door where Shelby left it. It will do for a lead rope, since John is wearing his halter, and save me going all the way out to the barn. I sling it over my shoulder and trudge around the house to the lower lawn. It's a hot, still, sunny day, and the grass feels cool under my bare feet as I walk down the slope. I climb over the stone wall at the bottom and then stand still, peering through the scrub growth of sumac and barberry for a glimpse of John grazing at the edge of the pond. If he hears me coming he'll move around to the far side, and it'll just take me that much longer to get him.

But I don't see him. He must already be around on the other side. I take the narrow path down to the pond, which looks very inviting today, blue and clean, without the scum that will cover it later in the summer. A glossy-necked mallard is peacefully afloat on its calm surface, bill tucked down into his breast. But of course the pond is no good for human swimming, too shallow, and all mucky underneath.

Ann McDermott asked me to come swimming at her pool today, along with a bunch of other kids, but I didn't feel like it. Now I wish I'd gone. A swim would feel good. Besides, what am I doing here anyway, tramping around in this heat, looking for somebody else's horse? I should have waited and made Shelby go after him for once.

There's a rustle among the thick reeds opposite me. John? No, a huge turtle, a snapper probably, heading down to the water. But then I hear the familiar sound of a horse blowing through its nostrils, and make out a patch of brown beyond the reeds that must be John. Resignedly I skirt the pond, picking my way around to the left through bleached saplings and rotting branches left by the spring flood. Bare feet and snapping turtles are not a good combination, as Dad has warned me more than once. I force myself to keep an eye out for more turtles. The mallard sees me and swims unhurriedly to shore to join his family concealed among the reeds.

I edge around a clump of reeds as tall as my head, and, sure enough, there in the grassy hollow beyond is John, feasting greedily beneath the shade of a big swamp oak. Trust John to make himself comfortable, I think. Well, it's for the last time; no such feasts will be coming his way at the riding academy, that's for sure.

The thought makes me hesitate, but only for a moment.

"Okay, John," I say, walking over to him, "the party's over." He raises his big head and looks at me, unconcerned—pleased to see me, if anything, in his dim way. "Stupid oaf," I say, and snap the leash to his halter that was once a bright red but is now faded and frayed by weather. Pam will give him a new halter at least, I think.

I let him have one more mouthful of rich grass and then lead him over to the right, where a strip of open land runs back uphill to the grazing field. I can't take him back the way I came, of course, and it's a long way around in the hot sun. I decide I might as well ride him back to the paddock and look around for the big rock I've used before as a mounting block. I've just heaved myself onto John's broad back when I hear a voice crying faintly, "Jessica! Jessica, where are you? Here, Jessica!"

Miss Emory, I think, out looking for one of her raccoons, though I didn't know she had one named Jessica. What a dumb name for a raccoon. I dig one heel into John's side, turning him uphill. I have no desire to get mixed up with Miss Emory and her raccoons today.

But the voice comes closer, and before we can get out of sight Miss Emory is hailing me from the top of the slope beyond the hollow, where the woods begin—a small gray-haired woman in a bright blue pantsuit, waving frantically at me. Reluctantly I turn and walk John back toward her.

Jessica is a cat, it seems, not a raccoon.

"It's moving day, they're all ready for me, and I can't find the dratted cat anywhere," Miss Emory says

131

breathlessly and then pauses. "Why, it's Katherine, isn't it? I didn't recognize you, you're so grown-up these days." She peers down at me with the sharp, inspecting gaze that hasn't changed since my fourth-grade days, any more than her insistence on calling me Katherine.

"And that's a new horse you're riding, isn't it? My, he must be gentle if you can ride him bareback and without any what-d'you-call-it, any bridle—heavens, I don't know where my mind is today, I'm in such a fuss. Anyway, not like that skittish white horse you had before. I used to positively tremble for you every time I saw you go by on the road. . . . Are you sure you haven't seen Jessica? A tabby, with three white paws? Usually she doesn't stray this far, but today she knows something's up—cats always do."

Something she's said finally registers. I release my hold on John's halter and let him graze again while I stare at her. "Moving?" I say. "You've sold your cottage?" Miss Emory nods, still looking around distractedly for her cat. "But what about the raccoons?"

"Oh, they're gone already—to that nice children's zoo over in Eastfield. They'll be well taken care of there, and of course they love children. . . . Don't look so sad, dear, it's for the best, really. I won't say it was easy parting with them, but now that they're gone—well, I confess it's something of a relief. I didn't realize how tied I'd become to the creatures, my whole life revolving around them all these years. Now I'm as free as a bird. Except for Jessica, that is." She calls the cat again, turning toward the woods and clapping her hands.

"Then—then they didn't force you out?" I ask stupidly. "The developers, I mean?"

"Well, in a manner of speaking." Miss Emory turns back to me and gives an unexpected chuckle. "That's what they'd like to think, anyway. But the truth is, dear, that I'm walking away of my own free will, and taking all their lovely dollars with me. I've always wanted to travel, and now I can. I've found myself a nice little efficiency apartment down in Norwalk to use as a home base, but I don't plan to spend much time there, not for a few years, at least. My sister will always take Jessica when I'm away, so. . . ." She stops, her eyes searching my face again. "Katherine, what's wrong? You look utterly miserable, and I'm sure it's not just because of my raccoons. I've always thought of you as such a happy child." When I just shake my head she says lightly, "Goodness, here I've been rattling along about myself when I meant to ask you about the other horse—the white one."

She waits—her intuition, too, as sharp as ever.

"He only looks white from a distance," I say, as if it were important somehow to set this straight. "Actually he's a dapple-gray. And— And I've sold him."

"I see," she says, though she can't possibly. "Well,

I imagine he was something of a handful." After a pause she adds gently, "I should think you'd feel just a little bit relieved—don't you, Katherine? Not to have the responsibility any more, I mean. Like me with the raccoons. And at least you have this other horse, who seems so calm and, well, biddable."

"He's just stupid," I tell her angrily. "And anyway, he's not mine. And I *don't* feel relieved about Tracker, I feel—"

I stop because I'm close to tears. Miss Emory sees that—you never could hide anything from her—and says in a matter-of-fact tone, "Well, dear, just think of all the other things you'll be able to do now that you won't be spending so much time riding and caring for horses. All the other interests you can develop. I've always thought you had a great deal of ability, Katherine—a good mind and a talent for getting along with all sorts of people. Oh, yes, that's the kind of thing you can spot, even in fourth-graders," she says with a smile. "Why, I remember when—"

"Goodbye, Miss Emory," I interrupt, unable to hear any more. "I hope you find your cat. I hope the raccoons will be happy in their cage, I hope you enjoy your traveling, because who would want to live in this rotten town anyway if they could help it. I hope— I hope the whole place just goes to hell!"

I wrench at John's halter, dig my heels into his grass-bloated sides, and wheel away from her. At a hard slap on his rump John breaks into his lumbering canter, and in a moment I have put Miss Emory out of sight behind me. I am sweating, and so, after a while, is John.

In the end I don't put him in his stall after all. His last full day here, and Tracker's . . . I can't. Instead I drag the boards from the shed and find the hammer and some big nails and begin slapping a makeshift barrier across the gap in the fence. I am still hammering when Shelby rides back in on Tracker. She calls something to me, but I pretend I don't hear. I don't look up.

13

The Gainesville horse show is still just held in some-body's field, but as Pam said, it's been getting bigger and more important in the last couple of years. Now there are even stands for the spectators on either side of the ring. Instead of trestle tables laid out with homemade cakes and brownies and pitchers of lemo-nade, there are regular concessions selling hot dogs and soft drinks and beer on tap. Out on the road a policeman is waving cars into a field across the way because all the extra space here is taken up by trailers and vans and the impromptu shelters people have rigged up for their horses and tack under the trees.

When I called Larry last night to ask if he could give me a ride over to the show, he said, "Kate— what in *hell?* I should think that's the last place on earth you'd want to go."

"It is, in a way," I admitted, and took a deep breath. "But . . . well, I'm not too proud of the way I've been acting lately, Larry. And my parents—"

"If this is some idea of your parents', then they can go with you themselves," he exploded.

"I don't want them to. It would look—well, it would look like they were forcing me." To Shelby, I meant. But I didn't want to go into that just then—the way I've been avoiding her ever since the horses left, refusing to answer the phone when she called. And she has called, quite a few times. "Anyway, my parents hate horse shows," I added. When Larry stopped laughing I said, "Please, Larry, I'd really appreciate it, if it's not too much trouble. Just a ride over. I'm sure I can hitch a ride back with someone."

"No," he said. "I mean, I'll stay there with you."

"Oh, Larry, you don't have to do that—"

"I know, but I will. Hell, I don't have anything else on my social calendar for tomorrow." His tone was bitter in a way I'd never heard before; after a pause he said, "I guess you don't know. Rita's split. To get married, of all things. She's gonna settle down and

137

be a nice little suburban housewife. Babies and self-cleaning ovens, the whole bit."

He was trying to sound casual, but there was a painful crack in his voice. I asked a few cautious questions. It seems that Rita ran into an old boyfriend from her college days, a medical student she'd almost married, except that she got scared and didn't. "The big commitment, all that crap," Larry said. "But now she feels mature enough—her word—to handle it. And so does he. Well, a hot-shot Establishment doctor, what else would you expect? Maturity's the name of that game, you better believe it."

Oh, Larry, I thought sadly. *You* could have asked her. So Rita wants babies and maybe even a decent kitchen for a change—"suburban" and "housewife" are just labels. They'll never have anything to do with Rita herself, with the kind of person she is.

He brought the subject back abruptly to the horse show. "I still don't see why you want to go, Kate. I mean, if you're just trying to prove something—"

"It's the right thing to do," I told him flatly, and hoped he wouldn't hear all the hours of lost sleep in my voice. "Besides, I've never seen Tracker in a show before. I think I should—just once, at least."

So here we are, on a perfect day for a horse show, cool and sunny, more like September than July. And so far the draft beer is the only thing Larry likes about the whole scene. He takes a swallow from his plastic cup and stands scowling at the bright crowd milling around us—the well-dressed parents and their friends, the riders in immaculate habits and shiny boots, the glossy horses. "I thought you said this was a show for *kids*," he grumbles.

"Well, it's a junior show, but that means anyone up to eighteen can ride in it." It's true that the only other time I was here, three or four years ago, most of the riders weren't much older than I was, and there were as many gymkhana-type events as there were regular classes. It doesn't look as though they'll be running any egg-and-spoon races today, that's for sure.

The loudspeaker gargles out something I can't understand, announcing a class. "Come on," I tell Larry, "let's go look at the outside course. Shelby's next class won't be for a while."

She's already ridden in one, an equitation class this morning, in which she took a third. We weren't here for that, but I know because Mrs. Peterson told us. She spotted us the moment we arrived and came hurrying over to me and gave me a hug. "Katie! Hey, it's great of you to come. Shelby will be so pleased."

What has Shelby told her? But of course I didn't ask. She looked just as pinched and nervous as all the other mothers, smiling a big fake smile as she told me about the equitation class. Then she turned to look at Larry inquiringly. I didn't realize she'd never met him. With his tangled beard and old sweat-shirt, his paint-spattered jeans and rope sandals, Larry doesn't exactly look like your usual horse-show person. I introduced them, glad that Mr. Peterson wasn't around. But I don't think she even took in the name. She said brightly, "Oh, are you another horse nut?" and Larry said, "No, just here to lend moral support."

Mrs. Peterson's eyes were already darting here and there, sizing up Shelby's competition, and she missed his tone. She said vaguely, "Well, I'm sure Shelby will be glad to have it."

Larry said, "I meant Kate."

Then she did hear him. She swung back to face him and her eyes were hard and she wasn't smiling any more. She said, "Listen, it was a business deal, fair and square. Kate knows that."

"Sure," Larry said tightly. "Long live business."

I tugged at his arm then and managed to get him away. Now, as we stand at the edge of the field watching the big hunters take their fences, I say, "Mrs. Peterson is really right, you know, Larry. I mean, for them it *was* just business. They wanted a better horse for Shelby, and there was Tracker, that Shelby had already been riding and showing, and . . . well, it just made sense."

I pause while a big roan with a boy rider surges over the jump nearest us—a thick, prickly-looking hedge—and thunders on by, finishing the round. I say earnestly to Larry's glum profile, "Look, Larry, I really appreciate your coming with me today and everything, but—well, don't think you have to stick up for me or protect me or anything like that. I'm here because I want to be."

"It's still got to be an ordeal for you," he says somberly.

The real ordeal was a week ago when Shelby and Pam came to take the horses away. But I can't talk about that yet, or maybe ever. I had an apple in my pocket for Tracker, but he never even nosed it out, he was so intent on everything that was going on— the van standing there, the bustle in and out of the tackroom while Dad and Pam sorted out the gear. It was old John who rubbed his head up against me and found the carrot I had in my other pocket for him; and it was John I hugged before I ran away back to the house and shut myself in my room and didn't come out again, even when Mom called up to tell me they were leaving.

Larry starts to say something, but stops as another enormous horse clears the hedge and gallops by—a powerful black whose rider is a slightly built girl about my age. She is obviously having trouble controlling him; he swerves and fights the bit as she tries to slow him and head him safely toward the exit. "Good grief," Larry says, staring after them. Just then someone takes a tumble on the far side of the field, coming

141

off a fence. In a moment he—or she—is up and walking around, but I see Larry glance over at the ambulance parked beside the stands and shake his head.

"The falls usually look worse than they are," I tell him, and add, "and at least this is a more—well, natural kind of riding, don't you think? More than in the ring, I mean."

"If you hunt foxes," Larry says with a shrug.

I know he feels I gave in too soon. More than that, it's as if I've let him down in some way. I tried to explain about that last terrible ride on Tracker, and how it made me realize what I was doing to him— forcing him to be something he wasn't, and maybe wrecking him for good. I didn't mean only the barbed-wire cuts, which are just faint scars now; I meant his whole nature, the special coordination of brain and nerve and muscle, everything that makes him a good horse.

But I don't think Larry understood. I'm beginning to realize that he doesn't really know or care any more about horses than the Petersons do—about horses as animals, I mean. They're an idea, that's all, that you make fit in with your other ideas about the things people ought to want out of life, and how the world should be. Boxes. I've been thinking a lot about Mr. Schuller's boxes lately. People shut up in stalls, maybe, like horses, their vision limited to what they can see over the top of a closed stall door. . . .

142

I don't like thinking this. It makes me feel disloyal to Larry. After all, he may not care anything about horses, but he does care about people—about me, for instance. He wouldn't be here if he didn't.

There's a spatter of applause from the stands, and the loudspeaker blares again through a crackle of static. Somewhere a baby is wailing. A helicopter whirs noisily overhead, a car horn gives off a long angry blast from out on the road. Larry gestures around us and says, "Doesn't all this racket bother him—Tracker? If he's as nervous as you say—"

I shake my head. "Shelby says it doesn't. I guess he likes being around all the other horses, and the excitement and the feeling of something special happening. And it's not like the noise is just for him. I mean, he wouldn't take it *personally*, the way he does on the road."

This makes Larry laugh. I'm glad to see him looking more cheerful. I hesitate, and then say, "Look, if you don't mind, I think I'll go over and say hi to Shelby and wish her luck. This next class is a big one for her. She's entered in another jumping class later on, but this is the one Pam thinks she has a good chance to win."

"Sure, go ahead. I'll meet you at the stands." He gives me a searching look and then smiles faintly. "Honest to God, Kate, you're too good to be true."

But of course I'm not. As I work my way through

the crowd toward the place under the trees where I spotted Pam's van earlier, there's a bitter, sour taste in my mouth that isn't just from the limp slice of pickle I ate with my hot dog. How will I feel seeing Tracker with Shelby, knowing that he belongs to her now, that he's nothing to do with me any more? Will I be able to speak the words I know I have to try to say?

Pam has brought several other horses to the show, and at first I don't see Tracker among them. Maybe I'm too late, I think hopefully, maybe Shelby's already saddled up and waiting on the far side of the ring for her class to be called. Then I see Mr. Peterson's tall blond head beyond the van, and when I come around it there they are. Shelby is giving a final grooming to Tracker's coat, which already gleams like polished steel, gray on lighter gray. His head is up, his ears pricked forward. He looks alert, ready for anything, but not tense. At the sight of him I find myself smiling in spite of myself, the way I smiled when I first saw him three years ago.

"Hey, Tracker," I say softly, and his head comes around, he blows through his nostrils; and then, as I stroke his neck he takes a strand of my hair in his teeth and tugs it playfully, the way he sometimes used to do. "At least he still remembers me," I say as lightly as I can, turning to Shelby. But I can hardly see her, my eyes are so blurred with tears.

144

"Well, Kate!" Mr. Peterson comes over and shakes my hand vigorously. "What do you think of your old horse now? Looks pretty good, doesn't he? And just wait till he gets in that ring. My girl here's going to show 'em just what he can do." He looks bigger and more self-important than ever, wearing his usual checked shirt but also some new-looking whipcord pants that could be, but aren't quite, riding breeches.

"Dad," Shelby says in a careful voice, "why don't you go along to the stands now? Mom's saving you a seat, and Kate can help me saddle up. Besides, if you polish that bridle any more there won't be any leather left."

"Well—" He hesitates, looking from one to the other of us. "Sure, guess I might as well. Good luck, kiddo." He gives Shelby a hug, and then slaps Tracker on the rump. Tracker is cropping grass now, and ignores him. "You just do like my gal tells you, okay, boy?" he says, as if Tracker were a small child or a puppy or maybe a wind-up toy.

He strides away, and Shelby turns to me with a little grimace. "Don't mind him," she says—and her blue eyes, looking directly at me for the first time, add, "Please." "Mom told me you were here, but I didn't know if . . . Well, anyhow. You don't really have to stay and help me if you don't want."

Shelby's hair is braided and drawn back from her face to make a shining coil at the nape of her neck.

In her dark breeches and boots and powder-blue coat she looks very sleek and pretty and sure of herself. But the leaf-dazzle of sunlight that strikes gold from her hair also shows me the slight quiver around her mouth; and suddenly I remember Shelby as a little girl, sitting fearfully on Max's broad back, clutching his mane for reassurance as I urged him forward. A moment ago I wanted to say something hard and mean to her, but I find I can't—any more than I could suddenly start yelling at Tracker.

She has picked up the bridle and is fingering it, her head bowed. "I guess you think I've been—well, sort of crude about this whole deal," she says in a low voice, haltingly. "But I thought if you had to sell Tracker. . . . I thought you'd *want* me to have him, instead of some stranger. Only now— I don't know, it's like I've stolen him from you, or something."

Unwillingly, I recognize the echo of something my father said a few days ago. "I don't believe in good losers," he said. "I think if you care deeply about something, losing it cuts you to the heart, and there's no point in pretending otherwise. But at least have the grace—the good manners—not to take your feelings out on the winner."

Good manners again. He had just come back from seeing Mr. Schuller, who, Dad thinks, has cancer and probably not much longer to live. Mr. Schuller was polite, Dad said, and in his odd formal way seemed grateful to Dad for coming, but as usual would say little about himself. I guess we will never know now just what it was he needed to keep for himself so badly—the thing that made him build himself a box and live walled-up inside it.

Luckily, Dad doesn't know about Miss Emory and how rude I was to her. I've been feeling bad about that, because of course the reason I got so mad was that she was right. About the feeling of relief, I mean—knowing I didn't have to worry about Tracker any more, that I would never again have to force myself to ride him against both our wills. I'm ashamed to admit that, but it's true. But mixed up with the feeling of relief is something else . . . a feeling of emptiness, of waiting for something. Waking up in the mornings, especially, I look out my window at the paddock, where there are no horses any more, and I think: what now? what next? These are scary questions because I have no answers to them. It's as if I'm standing in the middle of a huge empty field that stretches to the horizon. There's nothing to limit my view, whichever way I turn. No box, no walls. Is that it? But doesn't everyone need at least one wall at their back, a shelter of other people and caring?

Shelby is still waiting for me to say something. Even

Tracker seems to be waiting. He's raised his head and is looking from one to the other of us with his big glowing eyes.

"It's okay," I say, and suddenly I don't have to force the words. "I do want you to have him, Shelby. I guess I've been acting like a—what do you call it—like a dog in the manger. Or a horse in the manger, maybe." I find I'm actually able to smile again too. "Anyway, I want you to make the best of him. Of course I expect a blue ribbon every time."

"Oh, of course."

Shelby smiles back at me, and it's all right, we don't have to say anything more. In silence we go through the familiar motions of bridling and saddling, checking the girth and leathers. I help Shelby fix her number to her back; she settles her hat just so, and I give her a leg up into the saddle. I take Tracker's reins, and together, the three of us, we make our way over the trodden grass beneath the trees, past the vans and tethered horses, back to the noise and confusion and excitement of the show.

"Oh, wow." Larry leans forward, smiling a little. He takes off his glasses, wipes them quickly, and puts them back on again. "He's really going good, isn't he? And the way she rides him—like she has all the time in the world—like there's no one else *in* the world. . . ."

I watch Shelby fold forward, her weight perfectly centered on Tracker's back as he curves over the high white fence, front knees bent, taking momentum from the powerful thrust of his hindquarters. I don't bother to explain to Larry that it's the horse that's being judged in this event, not the rider, because how can you really separate the two? The smile on Larry's face isn't just for Tracker, it's for Shelby too, the way the girl and horse look right together—doing their thing, as he would say.

Shelby was nervous to begin with, I could tell by the way she licked her lips once or twice and squared her shoulders unnecessarily, as if to adjust the smooth fit of the blue coat. The first time around Tracker knocked down one bar and ticked another, but that was good enough to get him into a jump-off with two other horses. Now they've already had their turns. The first horse suddenly lost its rhythm and had two knockdowns. The other finished the round with just one touch, which should be good enough to win, but won't be, the way Tracker is jumping now.

A tight turn, and two fences to go. Shelby brings Tracker almost to a dead stop, and then puts him into the slow, collected canter I've watched them practice so many times. I hardly have to look to know that the jump will be clean, and the last one too. I think everyone knows it by now; you can feel it in the held breath of the crowd.

A perfect round. There is a solid burst of applause, and the satisfied murmur and nodding of heads that say, that's right, that's how it should be done. Larry feels it too, I can tell by his expression, absorbed and thoughtful as he too bangs his hands together. As for me, I am trying not to cry—not because of winning or losing, not because of anything at all except the way they looked so beautiful, the girl and the horse together.

Larry gives my arm a little shake and nods toward the center of the ring. They are awarding the ribbons now, and Shelby is looking around for someone: me. Her face is as composed and aloof as ever—Shelby will never do anything so childish as smiling (or scowling, for that matter) in the show ring, she will take whatever comes as if it's only her due—but as her eyes meet mine she gives a tiny nod. She leans forward and touches the blue rosette the judge has just pinned on Tracker's bridle. Then she holds her hand out to me, palm upward. I know what she is trying to say. The blue ribbon is for me.

About the Author

MARY TOWNE was born in Brooklyn and was graduated summa cum laude from Smith College. She is currently a staff consultant for the Institute of Children's Literature in Redding Ridge, Connecticut, and is the author of a number of books for children and adults.

Boxed In was inspired by her children's experiences with horses and the Connecticut countryside, where Ms. Towne now lives with her husband and three children—"Always," she writes, "surrounded by more animals than I can keep track of."

TOW

Towne, Mary

Boxed in

DATE DUE	BORROWER'S NAME	ROOM NUMBER
OCT 15	Krista Johnson	6
NOV 2 8	K. Johnson	6
MAY 2 4 '90	Erica	3
APR 2 3 '92	Jessica	3
SEP 2 4 '93	Amanda Holtz	5
APR 9 '97	Kristen G.	2